GW00675937

# NOʹT MY
# BABY

A totally addictive psychological thriller
with a shocking twist

# ANYA MORA

**Originally published as**
*The Midwife's Mistake*

JOFFE
BOOKS

Revised edition 2023
Joffe Books, London
www.joffebooks.com

First published in Great Britain as *The Midwife's Mistake*

This paperback edition was first published
in Great Britain in 2023

Cover art by Nick Castle

ISBN: 978-1-83526-085-2

# CHAPTER ONE

My water isn't supposed to break while a storm rages, when my husband isn't on the island and as the power flickers from on to off. Darkness covers the cabin as I cling to my belly. I never imagined it happening like this.

But the last sixteen months have taught me that nothing in life goes according to plan. This isn't me being negative — I'm a realist. At least I am now. Before, I was the epitome of optimism.

Worry washes over me as I consider what kind of mother this will make me.

Ready or not, I'll find out soon enough.

Another contraction barrels through me, leaving me gripping the butcher-block countertop in the kitchen. "Oh God," I cry out. The pain is not entirely unfamiliar, but I had forgotten how bad it would be. I hate that I am alone. That was not a part of the birthing plan. I wanted a calming playlist on, my acupuncturist on hand and a water birth as I ease my child into the world.

My cell phone is just out of grasp, but I reach for it across the kitchen counter, desperate to hear my husband's soothing voice. Ivan. I need Ivan. Now, more than ever.

Once the pain of the contraction passes, I tap on my husband's name on the phone screen, calling him and praying for a clear cell connection.

There are many reasons to love living in the San Juan Islands. But Shaw Island has a population of two hundred, which means maintaining our cell towers isn't a priority. And in our cabin in the woods, near the rocky coast, our reception is shoddy even on clear days.

"Maggie?" Ivan answers my call in a chipper tone, oblivious to the situation. Which makes sense. He's been hosting a yoga retreat on Lopez Island the last three days and is probably zenned out of his mind. Completely unaware of the situation I am facing.

"I'm in labor," I whisper, putting the call on speaker.

"How far in?" he asks. He is married to a midwife; he knows the right questions to ask.

"I just checked," I gasp. "An eight, at least. I'm so close." Tears prick my eyes and fall down my cheeks. Why am I alone right now? "Too close."

"Oh, Mags, it's going to be okay. I'm checking ferry times now. I wish you would have called earlier."

I press my hand to my belly as the baby moves deeper, lower and closer. The agony bites through my thoughts, and I moan as I look for words. Finally, I gasp out, "I thought it was a false alarm. It's three weeks early. I took a bath and a nap and woke up in . . ."

My words are lost as my body writhes. The phone slips through my fingers, hitting the floor, and I drop to my knees.

"Magnolia? Mags!" Ivan's voice cuts through the contraction. "Babe, you can do this. You can handle anything."

I wish that were true, but he and I both know that isn't the case. The last time I gave birth, it ended in disaster, heartache and pain I wouldn't wish on my worst enemy. Yes, I got through it, but it didn't make me stronger. It's made me scared, weak and fragile. Not the woman I used to be. Not the woman I want to be.

Before I was a confident midwife, able to hold my own with my patients, myself and my marriage.

And now?

I groan as another contraction competes for my attention, forcing me to crawl across the hardwood floors on my hands and knees toward my bed. The cabin is small with two bedrooms and one bath. Cozy. Now I'm grateful for the tidy size as I move toward my bedroom, wanting to reach my supplies before I give birth.

Gripping the edge of my mattress, on my knees, I bury my head against the cotton duvet. In the distance, I hear Ivan on speakerphone. "Maggie, I'll be there as soon as I can. As soon as the ferries are back up and running, I'll be there. I'll call . . ."

His voice cuts out. The call drops, and I'm alone. Utterly alone in our windblown home on the shore of Shaw Island. The lights are still out, and the room is dark.

I have only one neighbor. Rooney is at least seventy years old with limited mobility, and his memory has been half shot due to the flask that is always in his flannel shirt pocket. He's not someone I can call right now for help. If I'm going to do this, I'm going to do this alone.

And God, of course. I am doing this. It is all I want. To be the mother of a healthy, living child.

Tears fill my eyes as the pain threatens to break me whole. But I've helped hundreds of other women through this. That fact gives me confidence that I can do this for myself too. Earlier, after my bath, I brought my birthing supplies beside me, along with towels and sheets. I fumble through my kit in the dark, the moonlight through the window guiding me to the scissors and the salves.

It's surreal. This isn't the first time I've been on my hands and knees, bringing a life into the world. Except I need this to end differently. I can't bear to birth another baby that has already passed, already gone.

As the pain wrestles through me, I pull off my nightgown, sweaty and desperate for relief. I run my finger between my thighs, feeling the scorching pain, the slick sheen of a head barreling out of me. I close my eyes, and I breathe.

I can do this. I can do this. I can do all sorts of hard things.

My therapist made me repeat that as a mantra after I lost Lucy.

"You can do hard things, Magnolia," Dr. Bryerson would tell me.

And I would repeat it in my sleep, while I showered, while I washed the dishes and while I went for walks. I breathed it in, and I breathed it out. *"I can do hard things."*

That mantra is going to be my saving grace right now. Today. I can do this.

I've done so many other things I didn't believe myself capable of. Like burying my daughter, like leaving the psychiatric wing of the hospital a year ago, like weaning off my meds when I got pregnant a second time nine months ago.

Like finding my way back to Ivan after our marriage had become a shell of what it once was.

It was all my fault. Losing Lucy broke me in ways I was not prepared for. But this, this will not break me. This will be my deliverance.

The pain is excruciating, clawing through me until I know there is no stopping it from coming. It's time.

I close my eyes and I push. I push as I've never pushed before. I am the only thing this baby can count on right now. I will not let them down.

The last time I gave birth, Hollis was at my side, holding my hand, helping me through it. She is not only my midwife but also my coworker and a dear friend. And now I don't have her. I don't have Ivan.

I only have my own strength.

And maybe it's perfect this way. Maybe I needed this moment, to go through this labor all on my own to teach myself a final lesson: that I am capable.

More than capable. I am a mother.

I push again and again, and then with a gush and a push, and a sigh of sweet relief, I cry this child out into the world.

4

We didn't find out the gender during an ultrasound. I wanted a moment of magic. And now I have it, as this squirming, screaming beast of a babe, still connected to me with the umbilical cord, is wrapped in my arms.

I look at her, and I see her, and I know her. I've always known her.

"Oh my God," I whisper, sweat and tears streaking my face, my soul. I kiss her face over and over again, reaching for my bag of midwifery supplies, wiping her nose and pressing her sweet little body to my chest.

"I got you," I say. "Mama's got you." And I do. I have her in my arms, at long last.

The adrenaline rushes through me, and my legs shake, but I still have a placenta to deliver. I take hold of a soft cotton blanket, wrapping my daughter in it; she needs to stay warm. There is a bassinet by my bed, and I crawl over, pulling it toward me, and then I place my daughter in the basket.

"It's okay," I say. "Mama is here," I whisper. She's writhing as I did just minutes ago. And I reach within myself, taking hold of what I need and pushing hard, closing my eyes, and recoiling because the birthing of this is just as painful as the baby I just delivered.

It's a mess. There's blood, liquid and a part of my body on the floor. I allow the placenta to pump through the umbilical cord, nourishing my baby as I attempt to clean myself. I run a towel between my legs, touching to see if I tore. I'm relieved to find that I didn't. I look at her; she is small, maybe six pounds. Three weeks early. Pink, screaming, alive.

So, so alive.

I've done this hundreds of times for other women, cleaning up after they've given birth, so I'm not intimidated by the smells and the secretions. This is okay. This is more than okay. This is my literal heart's cry and song, all wrapped up into one perfect beat. She's mine.

I kiss her again and again and again as I lift her from the basket and draw her into my arms, wrapping a blanket around us both in my bed. I offer her my breast as tears fill my eyes. She suckles in the colostrum that is hers. All of me is hers, and she is mine.

Finally, I have a living, breathing baby in my arms.

Tears fall down my cheeks as I think of Ivan missing this moment. Knowing how unfair this is after everything he has been through. He's been at my side for the last year, and now he has missed this.

There was so much fear that we faced on a daily basis, not knowing how this pregnancy would end after the trauma we endured with the result of the last.

But I can't dwell on the fact that my daughter's father isn't here right now. I'm only going to fill this moment with pleasure and pride.

"You're perfect," I whisper.

She has a head of fair hair, chubby cheeks and a nose that's upturned. She's a mirror of me. A reflection I feel I don't deserve.

"I love you," I say. "I've waited for you." I wrap her again, carefully swaddling her in a blanket, exhaustion surrounding me. I put a tiny, creamy-white knit hat on her head. Then I place her in the bassinet by my bed so I can clean myself up. I gingerly walk to the bathroom in our room and turn on the sink faucets, letting the water run warm. I run a soothing towel over my tender places, place a pad in my underwear, and then put on a clean button-up nightgown.

In the kitchen I pour myself a giant mason jar of ice-cold water, drinking the entire thing at the kitchen sink before pouring a second and carrying it to my bedroom. I retrace my steps and grab an apple, biting into the hard flesh and moaning as I savor the sweet crunch as the juice drips down my chin. I wipe it away with my wrist as I reenter the bedroom, aching to hold her.

I pick her up again, wanting to never let her go. But as much as I want to cradle her in my arms on the bed, my eyelids are so heavy. My body is worn out. I need rest as I've never needed rest before.

There's no power, just the moonlight. There are no sounds inside, just the thundering storm on the roof. I pull my bedroom window open, letting in the scent of the sea through the screen. It envelops the room, covering us with a saltwater surrender. I lie in the bed, resting my hand on my daughter's chest. The rise and fall is the most remarkable thing I have ever experienced.

"I'll never let you go," I say, wanting to stay awake but unable to keep my eyes open for one more moment. I'll just sleep for a few minutes, I think, and then I'll hold her again. But she's wrapped up, safe and secure. And if she cries, I'll hear her in a moment.

I try as long as I can to stay awake, thanking God for her and praying that Ivan gets home soon. Soon. "Please," I whisper. "Come home."

My eyes fall shut, and sleep takes me.

* * *

When I wake, light is shining through the window. I'm disoriented at first, sore and tender in ways I've never been before. My body feels like I've been hit by a ton of bricks, and when I reach down to touch my belly, I'm shocked to realize and then quickly remember I gave birth last night.

Immediately, I look over at the bassinet beside the bed. It's empty.

"Oh God." Terror seizes through me. How did I sleep so long? It must have been hours. How did I not hear the baby wake up? Where is she?

"Ivan?" I call. "Oh God." I push myself out of the bed, my legs aching as I do, my thighs trembling.

"Mags?" Ivan.

He is home. Thank God. "Magnolia, Mags. I'm here. I'm here, babe." He is walking into the room, a swaddled baby in his arms.

I exhale, relief washing over me.

"I thought . . ." My words are a whisper, and I shake my head. "I don't know what I thought. I was scared."

"I'm right here," he says. "I got home an hour ago. That storm was wild. The ferry boat here from Orcas was down for a few hours. When I got home, you looked so beautiful, so peaceful. I don't think I'd ever seen you sleep so hard in a year or . . ." He pauses, not wanting to mention how things were a year ago, how they've been since.

How I've tossed and turned every night, waking up in nightmares, terrors and night sweats.

He moves to our bed and sits beside me. "You are so strong," he says. He leans down and kisses me softly.

Savoring the moment, I close my eyes, my breasts tender and aching. I need my baby pressed against my chest.

Also, I need to pee. I need to eat.

But first, I need to see her face again.

Ivan smiles down at me. "He's perfect."

I frown. "He?" I say. "He who?"

"Our son."

I shake my head. "I didn't have a boy. We had a little girl, Ivan."

His brows furrow. "Mags . . ." He tilts his head to the side. "Our baby isn't . . . a girl. You had a boy."

# CHAPTER TWO

Ivan looks at me as if I'm a stranger, a ghost, a shell of who I might be, might have been.

"What?" I ask. "Why are you looking at me like that? Just give me our little girl." I reach for the bundle of perfection in his arms.

"Mags." He shakes his head. "You had a boy, a baby boy. You didn't have a little girl. We have a son, Maggie," he says, sitting on the bed next to me.

I look at him with confusion. I feel it, too, in my chest, a tightening, a fear, a knot.

I take the baby from his arms, my baby. Sitting up in the bed, I begin to unwrap the swaddling, but before I even get that far, I look into the face of this child, this child my husband just held out to me.

My breath catches; my chest tightens. No.

This child is not mine.

"Ivan, this isn't . . . This isn't our daughter."

"I know," he says softly, tears in his clear-blue eyes. "Maggie, we lost our daughter. We lost her a year ago. I know you remember that."

My face falls, and I shake my head. "What are you doing? What's happening?" How did I sleep so long anyway?

I can't believe I could sleep for so many hours when I knew I was alone in the house with my newborn.

I look around the familiar bedroom, suddenly irrevocably scared, a ball of panic in my stomach, a knot in my throat. "Ivan, what are you talking about? I had a baby last night. Our baby, and this isn't her."

The way he looks at me is so filled with pity, so laced with sorrow. I pull back. My whole body is stiff. Looking at this child in my lap, not knowing what's happening, where I am, who I am.

"You need to calm down, Magnolia. Your words don't make sense."

My voice becomes high, and my throat dry. "Ivan, I'm not crazy."

"I never said you were crazy."

"I know, but I'm not. I know what happened last night. I was here."

"You were here alone in a dark house for way too many hours, having a traumatic experience, one you weren't prepared for in any way, let alone doing it on your own. We all were worried about how you would handle giving birth again. Dr. Bryerson, Hollis, everyone. We know what happened last time, and—"

"It's not like that," I say. "I remember it all. I remember it all so clearly."

And I do. I close my eyes, picturing the way I felt as the contractions ripped through my body, the way I fell to the ground, crawled to my bed and pressed my fingers between my legs as her head emerged into the world, our world. She took a breath, her lungs opening as she cried out, alive. She was here, and she was mine, ready for a life together. I held her in my arms.

Her, her, a little girl. I did not have a boy.

This boy, he is not mine.

I unwrap the blanket, staring at him, trying to piece together the truth of what he's saying. The baby in my lap is wearing a tiny, cream-colored kimono-style shirt freely allowing the umbilical cord to harden and a sage-colored cloth diaper. Both items are familiar. They are ones I purchased, washed and folded — then placed in the dresser drawer of the nursery one door over.

I unfasten the diaper, my fingers moving quickly, desperate to know if this is a little girl. It was so dark last night. Maybe the lack of lighting meant I couldn't see the face of the baby I gave birth to. Maybe the power outage meant tricks were being played on me.

But as I pull back the diaper, my eyes fill with tears.

Ivan's right.

This is a boy, a baby boy, who is perfect and beautiful. Rosy cheeks, sleepy eyes, but this is not the face of the child to whom I gave birth.

Five fingers on each hand, ten toes. I count them all. I look at his face. Blinking away my emotion, I look him over, desperate to see if he is of me, if he is mine.

I know he's not.

Ivan is pacing the room now, visibly shaken. "I need to call Dr. Bryerson. This isn't right," he says, a hand on his chest. "Hollis is going to be here any minute. Maybe she will know how to help."

"Hollis?" I say, realizing that, of course, she is coming over. She is a midwife, and I just gave birth. "Of course. But don't call Dr. Bryerson. We should call the police."

"The police?" Ivan stops, turning to me, his eyes pleading.

"Ivan, this isn't our daughter."

Ivan ignores my words. "I think she might be bringing one of the doulas with her from Homewood."

"Homewood?" I repeat, putting the facts together like Dr. Bryerson taught me. List the things you know are true to ground yourself back in reality, far from delusion.

I force the room to stop spinning for a moment as I put the pieces back together.

I worked at Homewood Midwifery with Hollis until a year ago. She lives on Lopez Island, not far from here. Donna

Smith is another midwife at the practice who lives on Orcas Island. The doulas who work with us to assist with childbirth are Melody and Clover. These coworkers were all my support people after I lost Lucy.

"Which doula is coming?" I ask.

"I think it's Clover," Ivan tells me.

I nod. Clover's twenty-six and happily married to Hunter and six months pregnant with her first baby. These are all facts. These things are all real.

This infant I am holding: the fact is it is not mine.

I don't know what I'm thinking, but I'm thinking this is wrong. Off. Something is missing.

"Ivan," I repeat, attempting to channel clarity. "This really isn't my baby. This isn't our baby."

There's a knock on the door.

"Look," he says. "Just calm down. I'll call the doctor. Okay?"

"I just need Hollis."

"No, you need your psychiatrist."

I don't need to talk to my shrink. I know what's happening. But do I?

How did a baby who's not my own end up in my husband's arms? Where did my daughter go?

But before I can process any of those what-ifs, Hollis is in our room with Clover on her heels. They're carrying a big basket of post-birth supplies.

"You did it, Mags baby," Hollis swoons. "I'm so proud of you." She wears linen pants and practical black clogs and a bulky brown sweater, and her salt-and-pepper hair is in a long braid over her shoulder.

"I can't believe you did this all on your own, Magnolia," Clover says. She comes over to me, sitting on the edge of my bed, wearing a pair of oversized overalls, her baby bump perfectly round and poking through the sides of the denim. "He's perfect," she coos. "Oh my God. What a night. Right? The storm was wild. The coast is covered with debris. The power is still out on Orcas. You're lucky yours is back on."

"Lucky," I repeat softly, not feeling lucky at all, feeling confused and lost and afraid. Who has my child?

"I'm going to give you a little checkup, and while I do, maybe, Clover, you can take a look at . . . Well, does the baby have a name yet?"

"A name," I murmur. "No . . ."

"Well, you've got to call him something. It's your little one now," Clover says. "He looks like a pretty hardy, strong guy."

Ivan is beaming down at the little boy in my arms. "We have a long list of options, but we never hammered one out, did we?"

I don't want to say it out loud, but I don't want to name this child because this isn't my baby to name.

It's someone else's.

"Mags," Ivan says gently, his hand on my shoulder. "Are you okay? Are you there?"

"I'm here," I say, blinking.

"Okay," he says. "You just checked out for a second, and let's remember to take deep breaths, okay? In and out, okay?"

I look at him as if he is a stranger, too, and snap, "I'm not one of your yoga students, Ivan. I am capable of breathing on my own."

The room stiffens, and I know it is my fault. Trying again, I add, "I'm just really hungry, and I need to shower, and I need to nurse this boy," I say, my voice rising, stress releasing from all of my pores.

The three of them relax with my conciliatory words.

"How about we do one thing at a time? You're going to take a shower, and while you do that, Clover's going to give a checkup on your son and make you an appointment with a pediatrician. And Dad is going to make some coffee. Maybe some tea? A bowl of oatmeal? What do you want, Magnolia? Eggs? Porridge? Toast?"

"Oatmeal is fine," I say, as I hand the baby to Clover, pulling myself out of the bed.

"Oh God," I say, clutching my stomach. "Everything hurts."

"Do you need help in the shower?" Hollis asks.

I nod, knowing I do. I also want her to make sure I don't need stitches. I don't think I do, but last night was blurrier than I remembered.

In the bathroom, Hollis turns on the shower, letting it begin to steam. "You doing okay?" she asks as I press one hand against the bathroom wall, bracing myself as I undress.

I shake my head, tears falling freely in the privacy of the bathroom with my friend. "I'm not okay. I'm . . ."

"I think it's just a shock," Hollis says with understanding. "Everything happening like this, so fast, and all alone. I know you were hoping it would be more peaceful. You had a birthing plan. You wanted a water birth this time."

This time. I'm brought back to the last time. I swallow. "I don't want to think about that. I don't care that it didn't go as planned. It was all really beautiful actually. I felt strong in ways I haven't in so long. I did it, all on my own, and I was so brave." I step into the shower, and Hollis sits on the toilet, listening. "I'm just glad the baby's healthy. That she was healthy."

"*He* was healthy, you mean," Hollis says. "Not that I'm looking to gender identify. I'm just stating the facts. The child you gave birth to is assigned male at birth. I don't know if you—"

"No," I say, closing the glass door of the shower. "It's not that. It's . . ."

Hollis looks at me through the fogging glass. Her lips press tight. Her eyes crinkle in confusion. "Look, you've had a long night and a confusing morning. You need a shower, a moment to unwind your thoughts. All right? One thing at a time."

I am not sure if she is right about everything, but the shower feels essential. It's exactly what I need, at least what I need to start with. I wash my hair clean with my tea tree oil shampoo, scrub my face with a eucalyptus-rose cleanser and run a washcloth over my most sensitive parts. Everything is still very tender.

As the hot water reddens my skin, I replay the night. The birth itself was perfect, which is surprising, considering I was here alone in the dark.

But it's not the birth that's troubling me. It's the after. It's the now.

It's where the hell did my baby go?

After I shower, I run a comb through my long, blonde hair, rub moisturizer into my skin and look at my face in the mirror over the sink, repeating the mantra: I can do hard things.

But this is more than hard. It feels unhinged. I feel unhinged. I press my hands on the counter, holding on, not knowing what is happening, terrified of what it might all mean.

Back in bed, Clover tells us the little boy is six pounds, four ounces. "And he is a charmer too. He opened his eyes for me. Look at him," she coos. "He's absolute perfection. Blue eyes, just like Daddy."

I know she is looking for ways to be kind, but I bristle all the same. All babies have blue eyes. This does not identify him as Ivan's son.

Clover rocks him in her arms as Ivan comes in with a tray of food, coffee with cream, a bowl of oatmeal with chopped walnuts, fresh blueberries and a spoonful of brown sugar.

I get into bed, the down comforter across my lap, pillows propped behind me, a typical postpartum scene.

"Thank you," I say, taking in the warmth of the moment. Two of my closest friends beside me, my husband here. I am grateful. I am.

With a force, I push away the other words threatening to steal the moment. Like the fact that I am certain I didn't give birth to a boy.

"Your doctor's going to come pretty soon," Ivan says. "So why don't you eat up?"

I frown. "Why is Dr. Bryerson coming now?" I realize after I say it, why. Ivan is worried.

"He is one of your biggest fans, Magnolia," Ivan says. "And you need to talk to someone about . . . about your fears."

"So the ferries are all working, then?" I ask.

Clover smiles. "Yeah, we got on one this morning. There was no problem at all. I guess the Orcas boat wasn't down longer than an hour. The Lopez one was out the longest."

I nod, knowing Ivan was on Lopez last night. That makes sense that he took the longest to arrive. And the birth happened so quickly, I didn't even have time to call Hollis last night.

The food is nourishing, and I needed it. When I finish the bowl of oatmeal, my breasts are begging for some sort of relief. Asking Ivan for the baby boy, I take him in my arms wondering if maybe I *have* lost my mind.

He looks so unfamiliar, but maybe some other mothers feel this way. There is no instant bond with this child — but I do feel a profound need to care for him nonetheless. He is a newborn; he needs to be cared for. I can do this.

And regardless of my own emotional state, the baby is hungry and looking for something, rooting around, and I know what he needs. Milk.

I press the child to my chest, knowing that while he is not mine, it is still my duty. The only thing I can do right now is to care for him in the way he deserves. Until I find out the truth.

I close my eyes as he begins to suckle as if by magic he knew just where to go, and I suppose he did. That is the miracle of life. The intrinsic understanding of where one belongs.

Even if this child thinks he belongs to me, I know better.

Hollis walks out of the room with Ivan, Clover cleaning up the tray and carrying it behind them. "Do you need anything?" she asks me.

I shake my head. "I'm just exhausted," I say, remembering how I felt after Lucy's birth. The exhaustion that overtook me, then, was deep and demanding. I had no baby to hold, no head to kiss and nothing but grief swallowing me whole.

It feels different this time. There isn't a wave of sorrow this time but confusion.

Clover looks like she wants to say more, but she holds back. "Maggie?" she says finally.

"What is it?" I ask.

"You're going to be an amazing mom. Just stay steady. Okay?"

I nod, tears in my eyes, wondering how in the hell I'm supposed to stay steady when literally on my first day of motherhood, it feels like everything has fallen apart.

## CHAPTER THREE

House visits aren't the norm with my psychiatrist.

Usually, when I see him, it's me headed over the deep, dark-blue water of the Strait of Juan de Fuca, toward Orcas, the same place Clover lives. The San Juan Islands are a majestic place to live. Off the coast of Washington with Canada in its distance, it's a beautiful green oasis that has always felt like home.

After I finished my training as a midwife in Seattle, I was looking for a job and got hired at Hollis's midwifery clinic, Homewood. That was six years ago. Shortly after I moved here for the job, I met Ivan, who'd been a yoga instructor in the area for a decade.

He was hosting a yoga class for mothers-to-be, and he brought his flyer into Homewood. I offered to pin it to the corkboard, and we got to talking. He was warm and kind, asking me where I moved here from and how long I'd been a midwife. It was easy to talk to him. He was handsome and friendly and the sort of man who makes you feel desired. He looked into my eyes and asked me to have coffee during that first meeting.

Soon we were taking kayak rides on the Sound, going to local breweries for live music, where we would dance and laugh, or cooking slow dinners in his cabin with bottles of French wine and making love before the appetizers were even served.

I quickly fell in love with him and my life on the island. It was such a contrast to city life. In Seattle, I had a few friends but no family, which meant I spent a lot of time alone, an insignificant cog in a corporate metropolis. Moving here meant I had a community. I felt complete.

At times, the pace of island life feels slow, but when I travel from one island to the next, on the ferry system, it's always a bit of an adventure. Ivan and I live in the cabin he owned before we met, on Shaw Island. Shaw is the smallest of the islands, so when I get to go somewhere else with a main street or a bit of a downtown, I feel like I'm getting out and about. As a midwife who has traveled from island to island, I have had plenty of chances to avoid becoming stir-crazy.

This last year, though, after losing Lucy and then becoming pregnant again shortly after, things have felt different. I have been so preoccupied with being in perfect health for the baby, to ensure this pregnancy ends with a live birth, that I've become a bit of a recluse. I have spent so much time at home, nesting and preparing for my second chance at motherhood. Early on, I began looking forward to my midweek visit to Dr. Bryerson, because it was my opportunity to get a change of scenery.

But today I am not going anywhere.

Today Dr. Bryerson is coming here to see me, to meet this baby who is not mine.

Ivan enters the bedroom with a steaming mug of tea. It's a blend that Hollis left, he tells me, setting it on the bedside table. The nettle-leaf blend is one I know well; it's a part of the postpartum kits we give every new mother. He takes the baby from my arm and sets him down in the bassinet next to me.

Then he gets into bed at my side, wrapping an arm around my shoulder. "Talk to me," he says. "I feel like the whole day has been a whirlwind. Your reaction this morning was hard to process. I feel so confused and want to support you, Mags, but I am not sure what you need."

I look over at the baby boy, jaw tensing, unsure of how honest to be. Growing increasingly scared of what my reality will imply to him.

He keeps talking. "It seems like the visit with Hollis and Clover went well. Did it? I want to touch base before Dr. Bryerson gets here."

I nod slowly, tired and worn out but also terrified because I don't know what's happening. I just know whatever it is, it's not good. "The birth was perfect," I begin to explain. "I mean, of course, it wasn't *perfect* perfect. You weren't here, but the labor was bearable. It didn't break me. I felt so proud, Ivan, of doing it on my own. Of pushing past my fears." Tears prick my eyes, and Ivan sighs, now sitting next to me on the bed and taking my hand. He is being patient, his blue eyes searching mine.

"Ivan, our baby was born, breathing. She looked like a mirror of me, of us, ours." I smile, closing my eyes, thinking of last night after giving birth and cleaning everything up, how exhausted I was, but surging with an adrenaline rush. "There was an electric current running from me, toward my daughter."

I try to explain that to Ivan, but he looks at me with confusion. "I'm sorry," I say. "I feel like you don't believe me. Like I'm . . ."

"Baby," he says softly. "It's not that I don't believe you, it's . . ."

I press my lips together. "You think I'm crazy."

"I think you've maybe lost sight of a few things, is all."

I lift my eyebrows. "Like reality."

"I didn't say that," he says. "I just . . ."

"Whatever. You don't have to believe me."

"Can we just wait until we talk to the doctor?" he asks. "I don't want to argue with you, not on a day like this, not when you've just given birth. I'm finally a dad, a father. You're a mother."

"I've *been* a mother," I say tightly. "I've been a mother for a year, ever since—"

"I know. I didn't mean it like that. I'm just . . . Look, we have a baby that's healthy and alive, strong. Hollis said there's nothing wrong with him whatsoever."

I lift my hand, wanting to cut him off. "Ivan, listen to me. It's not us . . ." I start, then swallow down my words, realizing everything I say is just giving him more reason to think I've lost my mind.

"I'm going to let you rest," he says. "Drink this tea and relax. And when Dr. Bryerson gets here, I'll bring him into your room. All right? I'm going to take the baby for now so that you can get some sleep. I think you're still exhausted."

He leaves with the baby, and I lift the ceramic mug of tea to my lips to take a sip, but it's too hot to drink. I set it back down, looking up at the ceiling around our cozy bedroom that is full of books and plants: neon-green vines of a pathos trailing the shelves. The big, shiny leaves of the monstera arch high in the corner. There is a dresser I brought from my grandmother's house, a bedspread I found at a second-hand shop. I've never needed the newest, brightest, or most expensive items for my home. I wanted solid things with a story. I wanted to see the history of all of it.

I lick my lips, confused. Have I lost all the threads to my own history? My own story?

I close my eyes, scared, knowing in my gut I can't return to the place I was last year. The two months I spent in the psychiatric ward in Anacortes, pacing halls, crying through the night and refusing meds, haunt me.

Losing Lucy broke me, reshaped me and started my whole life over. Tears fill my eyes with memories of sitting in a cold metal chair, trying to explain in group counseling why life didn't feel like living, feeling as if the other residents couldn't possibly understand my pain. I felt alone, like my pain was the most cruelly inflicted and my cross to carry alone.

Eventually, I recovered and found words for my grief, but that time was bleak. I can't go back there. I can't go back to that hospital.

I repeat that as I fall asleep. But the dreams aren't sweet. It's a nightmare — me in a hospital gown, slippers on my feet — my hair a bedraggled mess and my eyes bloodshot. My sleep tormented.

* * *

When I wake, Ivan and Dr. Bryerson sit in our room. The afternoon light filters through the window, casting a glow about the room. I hear gentle instrumental music in the living room, the cabin is warm, and the woodsmoke smell of a freshly made fire is keeping our home extra cozy.

It should be one of the most sacred days of my life. Instead, panic is the overriding feeling coursing through my veins.

Ivan kisses my forehead and hands me the baby. "I think he's hungry," he says with a smile. "I'm going to let you two talk. All right? Do you need anything before I go?"

I shake my head. "No, I'm fine," I say before he leaves Dr. Bryerson and me alone.

Dr. Bryerson is a good man, smart and an educated psychologist who has really helped me out of a lot of pain. He is in his sixties, with an even temperament, fatherly. He wears a collared shirt and a tweed sports coat. The opposite of Ivan, who is in joggers and sweatshirts most every day for his yoga practice.

Dr. Bryerson is usually so confident. Today, though, he looks concerned. "Well, can I meet the boy?" he asks with a smile I know he has expressed just for the moment. His apprehension is palpable, which makes me question his ability to care for me. "Your boy, your son."

"Sure," I say, offering the child to the doctor. "But I don't think he's mine," I whisper. Dr. Bryerson studies me. I take a deep breath, then let it out.

I reach for the now cold tea and take a gulp, wanting to avoid an awkward moment, realizing it's too late. Everything I say will make him think I'm even crazier than he did all year.

"Look," I say, wanting to explain myself. "I haven't lost my mind. I'm just confused because last night I gave birth and—"

"I know, Magnolia." He offers me a genuine smile this time as he looks into the face of the baby, rocking him gently as he stands a few feet from the bassinet. "Your husband filled me in on last night, and I spoke with the midwife too."

"You spoke with Hollis?"

"Yes," he says. "She said the baby's healthy, that you are healthy, and goodness, isn't that a relief? It's been your biggest fear for so long that you would give birth again, and it would end up in heartbreak. But just like your mantra promised, like the words that we've been working on reminded you: *you can do hard things*, and you did. Look at you," he says with a nod.

He hands the boy back to me, and I unbutton my night-gown, offering him my breast. The letdown is enormous. A relief washing through me. The unexpected ease of caring for this baby is a thrill, but it is overshadowed by the fact he doesn't belong to me.

"You look well," he says as he sits in the flaxseed-colored armchair near the bed. "Rested. I'm glad Ivan's here. I know last night was pretty traumatic, giving birth alone."

I shrug, staring down at the baby. "It should have been, right? It should have been terrifying, but somehow I felt strong. I felt capable. I think being alone was the perfect thing. I remembered how strong I was, what kind of woman I was before."

I smile, recalling the way I held my baby as she entered the world. Her wet, squirming body pressed against my bare chest, how I held her, breathing her in, swearing I'd never let her go. And yet here I have.

Tears fill my eyes as I explain this to the doctor. "It's my fault she's gone. I was going to take good care of her, and now my baby's gone. I fell asleep, and someone took her. Someone has her—"

"Your baby is here," he says. "Right here, Maggie. Right here in your arms, pressed against your body. Your baby is here. You are here. It's okay."

He keeps repeating things, but they're nonsense. They're not true. It isn't real. This isn't my child.

"I'm not crazy," I say, flabbergasted and frustrated. How am I supposed to make anyone believe me?

"I never said you were." His words are calm and concise. He rarely gives in to my emotions.

"You're looking at me like you think I'm crazy."

"I'm looking at you with concern, with care. Because I care for you, Maggie, for you and Ivan and this new child. And while I care for your past and your pain, more importantly, I want you to have a good, happy life with this baby. I want you to form a bond with him, to create a healthy attachment and not push him away because he's not Lucy. This boy is not Lucy. Maybe naming him will help you grow more attached."

"That's not it at all," I say, shaking my head, frustrated. "That's not it at all. Why won't someone just hear me and say, 'I believe you,' and call the police and look for—"

Dr. Bryerson clears his throat. "Maggie, we need to be serious right now. If you keep talking like this, we're going to need to take serious intervention."

I laugh. "Right, because I must have lost all my marbles."

"I didn't say you have lost anything. But perhaps you have lost your way."

"You're going to lock me up if I keep telling you the truth."

He presses his lips together. "I've ordered a prescription for you, a pain reliever, a relaxant and a sleep aid. They can all be taken while nursing. You need rest. You need a clear, level head, and sleep is the fastest way to achieve it. Ivan has asked if he can hire the other doula, Melody, at the practice, to come stay here for a while, and I think that would be a good idea."

"Ivan wants Melody to stay here? Why?" I would much prefer Clover, but she is six months pregnant, and it would be probably too much of a burden. Melody, though, has never been particularly friendly to me. She is more pragmatic than Clover or I.

"Because what you need right now is a lot of support. If you don't have any family, we can call to ask for help. You're all alone, besides Ivan. He needs the support as well."

"I have friends," I say, thinking of my best friend who lives on the island. "Thea. I'll see her. She'll help me. She'll—"

"Yes, I'm glad you have Thea, but Thea has a baby. Remember her son, Arden? And she can't be responsible for you and this boy, day and night. She is a friend, not a nanny."

"I don't need someone to be responsible for me twenty-four seven. I can be responsible for myself. I'm a grown adult. I'm—"

"I know you are," he says more sternly now, "but Melody is going to come stay with you. She lives alone. She has the capacity to be here with you and Ivan. She's going to help make sure that you get plenty of sleep, plenty of hours of rest. She'll bring you the baby when he needs to nurse but will make sure at night that you get the rest you need. That's what's going to keep you healthy. What's going to keep you sane. What's going to keep you—"

"Out of the hospital?" I finish for him.

He nods. "Exactly. Sometimes we need tough love, and that time is here. Magnolia, you can do hard things. This might be hard because you're expecting this baby to be a recreation of Lucy. But the reality is you have a new baby, this new, beautiful boy who needs you as his mother. All right? Because if that doesn't happen, if you don't attach to this boy, if you don't do everything in your power to take care of him, to give him what he needs, that would . . . Well, it could result in . . ."

"Me going back to the psychiatric ward?"

"Yes," he says. "Those are just the facts. I'm worried. Ivan's worried. Hollis is worried. That's a lot of worry for the first day of your motherhood."

"It's not the first day," I say. "I've been a mother for a year."

He sighs. "I know. I know you have."

"But that's not the same as this," I finish.

"It isn't," he says. "What happened a year ago when you lost Lucy, when she came into this world, already gone, was a tragedy. A tragedy you got through, and now you're going to fight for something bigger or something better. Okay?"

I nod, letting his words take up all the space, because nothing I have to say matters anyway. I'm not going back to the hospital.

If I am locked up in a psych ward, there's no way in hell I'll be able to find my daughter.

And right now, that's the only thing that matters.

## CHAPTER FOUR

This past year, I haven't gone to work once. I took a long-term leave of absence after Lucy was born, and then after my stint at the hospital, I became pregnant within a month.

That was not a part of a plan, any plan, but it's life.

Getting pregnant again was terrifying. I didn't think I was strong enough to handle it, and to be honest, I don't think the people around me did either.

Everyone's been walking around on pins and needles for seven months straight. Everyone's been worried, and now I see none of that has changed. Worry rests on everyone's faces.

Ivan's looking at me with trepidation. Melody, the doula, who's been sent here to babysit, is watching me constantly. She came last night after the doctor left, and while she has been helpful, it also feels like a giant freak flag flying in the sky announcing my inadequacy.

I can't handle this on my own. And if I can't handle this, what else am I ill-prepared for? How can I face motherhood when this child, who everyone is saying is mine, feels like a stranger?

When I carried Lucy in my womb, I felt like I knew her. Like her heartbeat was my heartbeat. Her song, my song. Her life, my life.

I felt the same way throughout the pregnancy a second time, which is why it feels so strange and unfamiliar now to look at the baby and know intrinsically he isn't mine.

Even if I can tell myself I made this all up, that this baby in my arms is my child, I can't shake the feeling. The feeling like I've never seen this person before. Like I don't know him at all.

He suckles against me, and I'm grateful he has taken to breastfeeding. Not because I think breast is best or something obnoxious like that, but because I'm hoping this will bring us some sort of connection.

Yes, I can see how I am living a parallel reality, both saying this baby is not mine and is mine, but I don't know how to proceed. I don't know what I'm supposed to do. I feel insanity creeping around the corners of my mind. Crazed, like I'm the one who's lost reality.

Ivan has just showered and shaved. He walks out in a pair of black joggers and his tight-fitting tee-shirt, lean and strong. Smiling and radiating positivity. He is like home to me.

"What are you getting ready for?" I ask, sitting up in bed.

He cocks his head in confusion. "Mags, we talked about this. I have a three o'clock session with a private client, and I was going to drop you off at Thea's during it."

I frown, not remembering. "Really? When did we talk about that?"

"Over dinner last night."

I remember the butternut-squash soup and crusty sourdough bread slathered with butter. A glass of milk — something I never crave — ice cold and delicious. But I can't remember speaking to Ivan about visiting Thea. Still, I am grateful to see her. She understands me.

Ivan, though, is still stuck on the fact I can't remember the exchange about this outing. "How about tonight we let Melody do a little bit more of the heavy lifting? Magnolia, it worries me. We talked about this. We made a whole plan.

Thea is looking forward to it. Everyone thought it might be good for you to get out of the house."

"Is Melody coming with us," I ask? "I don't want her to."

"That's fine. She can stay back. I think you just need some girlfriend time, a chance to leave the house and shake it up a bit. You need to keep your head clear, honey. You need to keep your mind—"

"I get it," I say. "You think I'm crazy, and I need to find some perspective. Understood," I say with a sharpness I don't recognize as my own.

I place the still-unnamed baby in the bassinet I had bought for my new child, and I get out of bed.

First things first, I need to change my sanitary pad since I'm still bleeding. I look in the bathroom mirror, noticing that my deflated stomach isn't one I recognize. I shower quickly, braid my hair without drying it, and pull on soft, black leggings, a nursing bra and a pine-green cashmere sweater.

Dressed for the day, I begin to breathe. I exhale, thinking through the implications of this plan Ivan has made for us. While I'm not exactly ready to see Thea's son, Arden, who at sixteen months is one hell of a handful, I do know I need to process with my closest friend. And I would rather be with Thea than tiptoe around Melody, who I know is judging me, watching my movements in the house, for my lack of maternal connection with the infant in our home.

Thea and I met in a pregnancy yoga class back when we were both carrying our first babies. The class was one of Ivan's, and it was fun seeing him in that light, leading us in pregnancy-friendly positions. While I have taken numerous classes with him over the years, supporting his events and endeavors, I am not a yogi. I prefer to garden or take a walk to decompress, not stretch out in a sphinxlike pose. But the pregnancy had me craving chances to be with other moms-to-be, and this class had always been one of Ivan's more popular. After a few minutes in the class, I understood why. My body was growing and changing so quickly that being led through a series of stretches that would cater to my shifting body felt incredible.

Throughout the slow-flow class, Thea and I would catch each other's eyes and smile. A petite woman with curly black hair, she was my physical opposite, but we had so much in common with the current state of our bodies. We both groaned when attempting to move to our hands and knees for a cat-cow pose and laughed at the ridiculous idea of touching our toes.

After finding a quick camaraderie a few weeks in, we grabbed fresh juices at the place on the corner. We had a lot to talk about. For both of us, it was our first pregnancy. We detailed what our ideal birthing plans might look like, hoping the birth would be easy. How we felt huge, and how the yoga positions were impossible.

I'd laughed and told her I'd give Ivan her feedback.

She smiled. "Men can be impossible, can't they? My husband just got hired on the island as a police officer, but he hasn't made many friends yet, so he's always at home with me, and it can be a little annoying at times."

I laughed. "My job's always kept me on the go," I told her. "Being a midwife has me stopping at different islands and checking in with various patients, and Ivan works on the go. He's always hosting retreats and different classes and meeting with clients at other studios."

"That's kind of cool," Thea had said. "You both have pretty interesting jobs."

"What do you do?" I asked her.

She smiled. "Honestly, not a whole lot these days." She ran her hand over her big belly. "I'm just ready to have this baby. Before I got pregnant, when we were still living in Seattle, I was an IT specialist, but now I'm taking a leave of absence. Thankfully, Tanner can hold down the fort with his new position."

"That's why you moved up here?" I asked. "Because of his job?"

She nodded. "Yes. I had this image of this idyllic childhood on the island for this baby. Montessori education and playing in the woods and collecting seashells and snails." She smiled. "Silly, but I still want it!"

I laughed. "Not silly. My childhood was pretty rough, so I want the same things for my baby. I want this child to have the life I never had. One that is stress-free and happy."

"Well, our kids could grow up together. That is pretty cool to think about," Thea had said. "I bet being a midwife, you constantly meet incredible women raising families here."

"Oh, for sure. All the granola mamas in the Pacific Northwest gravitate up to the islands. I feel lucky to help them in such a monumental moment in life."

"You have to really appreciate the miracle of life to do a job like that, I'd imagine," Thea said.

I smiled. "I've always liked caring for people. For a long time, I thought maybe I would take care of older people. I was with my grandma for the last years of her life, but after she passed, I had this inkling of something new. For new starts, for the beginning. The endings are always so sad, you know?"

"Personally, not really. I have never lost anyone close to me. But I can imagine."

I couldn't imagine a life like that. I had lost my parents in a car crash when I was young and was raised by my grandma, who always struggled to make ends meet. Thea, though, felt like a breath of fresh air: she was buoyant, and nothing weighed her down. I needed a friend like that, who was not a part of my job as a midwife — who was there for me, without asking for anything.

"How did you find out about this yoga class?" I asked her as we finished our beet-and-celery juices.

"Oh, I read that lifestyle blog that Yardley Fields writes. I don't know if you know her, but she's an influencer who practices yoga. She lives on San Juan Island. Kind of embarrassing now that I'm saying it out loud. I'm not a stalker. I swear."

"I didn't think you were," I told her, meaning it. "She comes off as incredible with more people than just you. And God, she is beautiful, right? I work with a woman named Hollis, who owns the midwifery practice Homewood, and her sister is Yardley."

"That's a small world," Thea had said. "Have you met her?"

"Yeah. She's amazing, just like her sister. Only different. Hollis is down to earth; Yardley is a romantic."

"Do you have family?" she had asked me.

I shook my head no. "Which is why becoming a mom is so important to me. I want a family of my own. My parents died when I was young, and I grew up with my grandma, who, like I said, has passed on."

"And, Ivan, your husband, does he have family?"

I looked at her, surprised at her interest. Usually, a conversation with someone you've just met lasts a few minutes, and then they move on without digging deeper. But it was clear, right off the bat, that Thea was interested in me for me. I hadn't had a friend like that in a long time.

Sure, I got along with Hollis, but that's in a business sense. That's about the hustle, about the clients, about our patients. This felt different immediately. Thea felt like a friend, one I hadn't had in a really long time.

Now, back in the present, preparing to go to her home for a visit, I feel a rush of need to talk with her one on one. I look over at Ivan, who is dressing the baby on the bed. I realize that he's probably doing me a service by insisting I go see her today. Friends are good when you're having a hard time, and I think we can unanimously agree that it is exactly what I'm having.

I slip my feet into UGGS, and I watch as Melody buckles the baby into the infant car seat. I triple-check the baby bag, diapers, change of clothes, blanket and an extra hat.

Ivan smiles. "The only thing you forgot was to eat." He hands me a morning-glory muffin wrapped in a cloth napkin.

"Thank you," I say, kissing his cheek before looking down at the baby. "I guess it'll be your first car ride," I say.

Melody smiles at me. "Yeah, you're going to do great, Magnolia." She pauses, meeting Ivan's gaze before mine. "Would you want me to come with you?" she asks. "I could hang out with the baby while you're visiting with Thea or help her with her son, Arden."

"That's all right," I say briskly, not caring for her insinuation. "I'll be fine. I can handle watching my baby for an hour, but thanks."

Melody looks over at Ivan, shrugging as if I can't see her. A silent conversation between them, but I know exactly what they are saying with their eyes. She can't handle it. She's not capable. She's been broken before, and she's breaking again, but this time it's going to be a snap.

I pull in a deep breath and put on a brave face. "But thank you so much for offering, Melody. I really appreciate it. But since you've been working so hard all night, why don't you treat yourself to a nap while we're gone and help yourself to anything in the house? There's the bookshelf, games, puzzles and, of course, food in the fridge. Ivan and I can bring something back for dinner after our time in town."

Melody smiles tightly. "Of course," she says. "I'm not trying to annoy you. I'm just trying to help. Ivan and your psychiatrist and Hollis all asked me to be here, so . . ."

"I know," I say. "I'm not upset with you. I'm just trying to get through one moment at a time."

Melody smiles more softly now. "All right," she says. "Then go have fun and visit with your friend. Sometimes that's the best medicine."

In the car ride, I'm sitting in the back seat with the baby, terrified at the bumps and jumps as Ivan drives down the gravel lane.

"Slow down," I say.

He smiles at me through his rearview mirror. "It's nice to see you being maternal."

"I'm plenty maternal," I snap. My annoyance with Melody doubting my ability to do this outing has my less-than-lovely colors showing.

"Geez," Ivan scoffs, looking at me in the rearview mirror. "What is that about?"

"I've been nursing this baby, caring for him, holding him and rocking him, and then you act surprised that I am being a good mom? Honestly, it makes me feel terrible."

"I'm not looking to fight with you," Ivan says with raised eyebrows, stopping at a red light. "I'm just happy. It's nice to see you taking care of the baby. It's what you've wanted since I met you. And now you got what you wanted, right?"

"Sure," I say, knowing it's not the truth.

What I want is my daughter, my perfect little girl that I gave birth to in the middle of the night. She was the light I'd always wanted, and she is not here, and instead, I have this baby who is not mine.

When he pulls up to Thea's house, he helps unlock the car seat from the back seat and carries the car seat to Thea's front door. She has a cozy home, a two-story bungalow that's nestled in the woods. There are pumpkins on the porch and a wreath on the front door. When she pulls it open, I see a fire roaring behind her and her toddler at her heels. She picks Arden up, setting him on her hip in one fell swoop.

"Oh, Maggie. I'm so happy you're here," Thea says, wrapping me in a big hug and cooing as Ivan carries the car seat into her home. "I'm so proud of you, mama. Tanner's not home; he's working overtime," she tells Ivan. "Been crazy the last few days with that rainstorm."

"No worries," he says. "I've got to go anyway. I have a session with a client for the next hour. I'll probably be back in seventy-five minutes or so. Sound good?"

She smiles. "Yeah, we're great. No worries."

The way they look at each other tells me that they've been having conversations without me, and I'm not stupid. I'm sure I know exactly what they had been saying.

*Magnolia has lost it again.*
*She's lost her mind.*
*Please save her from falling off the cliff of insanity.*

I swallow down my annoyance at their apparent sidebars about me and instead follow Thea into the living room. Ivan has set the car seat on the coffee table, and she leans down to unbuckle him.

"Oh, Maggie, he is so handsome." Arden is next to her, and she sits down on the couch once the baby is nestled in her arms.

"I'll be off, then, Magnolia. Call or text if you need anything." He gives me a quick hug before leaving.

Thea's eyes take me in. "He is so concerned about you."

"I know. I have people hovering around me all day and night."

Thea laughs as she pulls off the baby's knit hat and runs her fingers over his full head of black hair. "Hovering? You just gave birth; everyone is right to be helping."

I sit next to her on the couch. "Melody is staying with us, the doula from the clinic. She drives me nuts."

"Just find your rhythm. Be thankful for the full-time help."

"Ivan thinks I am incapable."

She reaches for my hand. "We both know that isn't true. This is a big adjustment for him, too, especially with the current state of your mental health . . ."

"Please don't put me on the crazy train, too, before you've even heard my side."

She sighs, looking at Arden, who has returned to his wooden blocks on the carpeted floor.

Ignoring my comment, she changes the subject. "So you haven't named him," she states.

"Not yet," I say. I bite my bottom lip. "Hey, do you have any coffee?" I ask.

"Of course," she says. "I made the coffee cake too."

"Sounds good," I say, watching as she carries the newborn with her to the kitchen.

She starts talking as she enters the kitchen. "So, I didn't come by yesterday because it just felt like a lot was going on, but Ivan did call me and . . ."

"I figured as much," I say.

She pauses, looking down at the bundle of pure joy in her arm. Without meeting my gaze, she stares into the baby's round face.

Tears fill my eyes. This moment, where my best friend meets my baby, should be one of elation; instead, I feel a pressing weight on my chest, and I don't know how to stop it.

"Mags, are you okay?"

I answer shakily, looking out the window over her kitchen sink. An apple tree stands tall in the center of the yard, apples fallen on the grass. I feel like I'm falling too. "Can we not talk about it?"

"No," she says, with a shake of her head. "We literally have to talk about it. It's the only thing that I want to talk about, besides hearing about your miraculous birthing experience. Which, by the way, sounds like it was a Lifetime movie."

I groan as she hands me back the baby so she can prepare a pot of coffee. She grabs the half and half out of her fridge and then reaches back for the baby as the coffee brews.

"He's perfect, right?" I say, knowing it is true. Regardless of my truth, I know this boy is beyond wonderful. Whoever he belongs to must be heartbroken too.

"Precious and beautiful," Thea says, "because he's yours." She pours two mugs of coffee, slices the cinnamon cake on two plates, and then sets everything on a tray to carry into the living room.

"He's not, though," I say.

I see her body stiffen, and through her eyes, I see her thoughts race, as if she's picking her words carefully. Eventually, she says, "Maggie, if you go down this rabbit hole, I'm scared you're never going to get out."

"I'm not going down a rabbit hole," I say. "I'm not try-ing to be dramatic or panic or—"

"I didn't say you were, but Maggie, you've gotta know that this is dangerous, what you're playing at."

"I'm not playing at anything," I say, tears in my eyes, frustrated that she doesn't see eye to eye with me. But how could she?

We walk back to the living room. She sets the tray down on the coffee table, telling Arden, "Careful, no touch," before joining me on the couch.

Holding the baby in my arms, I begin to explain how the birth went, how perfect and miraculous it all felt. How, afterward, I felt complete in a way I never had before. Like all my fears were gone, and my deepest desire had come true. Instead of ending in heartache, it ended in pure happiness.

"And then you fell asleep?" she asks.

I nod slowly. "Yes, I slept so hard, which is wild. Should I have been more alert, considering I was all alone with the baby?" I shake my head. "And then I woke up, and the baby that Ivan was holding wasn't mine."

That's where she stops me. Cutting in, she says, "Magnolia, how would that even be possible? It was only, what . . . five or six hours from the time you gave birth to the time you woke up?"

"Yes," I say, having counted the hours myself. "But a lot can happen in five hours."

"On the night of a huge rainstorm that stopped several ferry routes?"

"Not all of them were canceled," I clarify.

"You're telling me someone stole your baby and replaced it with another baby that also is a newborn?"

"I know it doesn't make sense," I say, "but . . ."

Thea sighs, taking a sip of her coffee. "But you think it is true anyway?"

"There is no reason to even talk about this to you. Everyone thinks I'm on the way to the psych ward. You are no different."

"Why? Because I'm saying something hard that needs to be said?"

"No," I say. "You're my best friend. You're supposed to be on my side."

"Oh, I'm on your side," she says. "Sweetheart" — she takes my hand — "I'm on your side through all of this, through all of the ups and downs. Don't question that. I got you, but Magnolia, what you're suggesting is . . ."

"Insane?" I finish for her.

She gives me a wry smile. "I wasn't going to say it quite like that, but yeah, it's pretty unfathomable."

"Fine," I say, exhausted by the people around me who don't think my truth is worth exploring. "I'm sure you're right."

At this, though, Thea surprises me. Instead of agreeing that I've lost my mind, she shrugs. "But what if I'm wrong? What if this is your mother's intuition, and you know something the rest of us don't?"

My breath catches at this change in consideration. Relief washes over me for the first time since I gave birth. Someone has listened.

"So you'll help me find my baby, find my daughter?" I plead.

Thea's eyes fill with tears, and I'm torn, trying to read her. Is it pity or belief?

I decide I don't want to know the answer.

"I'll help you any way I can," she says.

# CHAPTER FIVE

When Thea gets up to lay Arden down for a nap, I pull the baby close and offer him my breast. He begins to suckle immediately, and I tell myself that I can do this. I can be the mom that this baby needs until I find his real mother.

This is the kind of thinking that Ivan and Hollis would be furious about, but I can't shake the feeling that I'm not crazy. If I say it enough, maybe that will make it true.

Thea returns to the living room with a refill of coffee. She launches into an unexpected story as the baby finishes nursing.

"So, did you hear what happened to that girl who works at the coffee shop over on Lopez Island?"

"What girl?" I ask.

"Billie? Billie Davis? Do you know her?"

I nod. "Yeah. She's one of Donna's clients." Donna is another midwife at Homewood, and she lives on the same island as Billie.

Thea nods slowly. "Right. She works at Swept Away; you know that cute little coffee shop?"

"Oh, I love that place. They have the best oat-milk lattes," I say.

Thea's eyes search mine. "She gave birth the other day."

"What day?" I ask.

"The night of the storm. She'd been living in an apartment over the café. Went into labor, the same night as you."

I nod. "Who told you all this?"

"Tanner told me," she says, referring to her husband, who is a police officer. "The thing is, Donna couldn't get there because they're on different islands, so Hollis came — they're both on Lopez. Anyway, it's so awful." She pauses. "Hollis didn't say any of this to you?"

"No," I say, "but what exactly is so awful?"

She exhales slowly, taking my hand in hers. "Her son died in birth."

As she says it, Thea and I both have the recognition of why Hollis kept this from me.

"I'm sorry," she says. "It's probably the most triggering thing I could have said, right? It just felt wrong not to."

"It's okay," I say, remembering the agony I felt when Lucy was not breathing, when I drew her close to my skin, praying for a miracle that never came.

"Is it, though?" she says softly.

Tears fall down my face, landing on the soft cheek of the baby in my arms. "I don't know," I whisper back.

The baby has started to fuss, and I switch sides. "So Billie's son was stillborn?"

"I think so. I don't know all the facts. I just heard about it from Yardley. She posted something in her Instagram stories about tragedy, and I messaged her, asking if things were okay. She told me about Billie. She'd heard of it from Hollis."

I nod. "Well, it makes sense why they wouldn't have said something to me. They think I'm completely fragile. Melody, one of the doulas at Homewood, she's living at my house right now. She came the day I had the baby and hasn't left yet. It's been forty-eight hours."

"Mags, I don't think that's a very long amount of time to get help. Hell, when I had Arden, my mom came up to the island for three months. I think it's normal — beyond that, it's supportive that your husband's making it a priority. That you're getting taken care of."

"It feels more like a threat," I say, "because he thinks I'm crazy. If I don't snap out of it soon, he's going to send me back to a psych ward. Dr. Bryerson said as much when he came by to check on me."

"Well, no one wants that," she says. "You have a baby you have to take care of. You can't go away."

Rolling my eyes, I try to connect with my best friend. "One minute, you're telling me that you trust me and think I should work on finding my daughter, and the next minute, you're siding with everybody else."

"There are no sides here, Mags," Thea presses. "There's life. There is a life right here in your arms and . . . I don't know. I'm worried about you too."

I sigh. "I just want one person on my side."

"I *am* on your side. We've been over that."

Switching back to Billie, I ask about her, "How is she holding up? She's pretty young, right?"

Thea nods. "Twenty-one, I think. Her and her boyfriend split before she found out she was even pregnant, so I think she's doing all this on her own."

"Damn," I say.

"I know. It's so sad, right?"

"That night was horrible," I say, "but I guess I'm glad Hollis didn't tell me right away. I might have become hysterical on Billie's behalf. Probably would've had one more reason for everyone to think I had gone crazy."

"I don't think you're crazy. I just think you're confused."

"I don't know if that makes me feel any better," I groan. I reach for the coffee and take a sip. The baby has finished nursing, and Thea takes him from me to change his diaper on the carpeted floor in her living room. She sorts through my diaper bag, picking out a clean cloth diaper.

"He still has his umbilical cord. He's so teeny tiny."

"I know," I say. "I can't believe it. Does it make you want another?"

She chuckles. "I hated being pregnant — and the labor? No thanks. I'm sure you feel the opposite, considering you were a glowing creature during the entirety of this pregnancy."

"When I gave birth, it was so exhilarating," I tell her. "It really was the opposite of what it had been like last time. I am so thankful for a second chance. I hadn't felt that empowered in so long, so fully capable."

Thea nods, tears in her eyes, remembering the last time. Everyone had come around to the cabin when contractions began. All our friends were so excited for us that they'd been in the living room, supporting Ivan and me, however they could: Thea and her husband, Tanner, and Donna and her husband, Keegan, our closest friends. They wanted to be there as I brought my baby into the world, and instead they were there as my world came crashing down around me.

"So what do you want to do next?" Thea asks. "Besides get some good sleep — which Melody will be able to help you with."

I shrug. "I don't know what I'm supposed to say anymore. I feel like anything I do or say will be held against me."

"That's not how it is between us. I'm your girl through thick and thin, for always."

Just then there's a knock on the front door.

"I bet that's Ivan," I say warily.

Thea nods to answer it, and in comes my husband, who is sinewy and strong, a smile on his face like he's just won a race. Yoga always does that to him. Zens him out and blisses him out and makes him clearer in the head. Maybe it's what I need, stretching to ease my discomforted mind.

"How did it go?" he asks Thea. He looks over at me and our baby lying on the floor.

"I was just changing him," Thea tells him. "He's so perfect, I could just eat him up."

Ivan nods. "You're telling me. I haven't been able to keep my eyes off this guy."

"You need to name him, though," Thea says. "We can't just keep calling him the baby."

"That's what I've been saying," Ivan says with an easy smile. "For some reason, my wife's resistant."

"You *know* why I'm resistant," I say tightly.

"Right," Ivan says with a faltering smile. I know he is so pleased to be a father, and the disconnect we both feel at this moment is overwhelming. We were supposed to be in this — in everything — together. "Well," he continues, "if you're not going to do the honors, I'm going to have to name him something."

"What are you thinking, Ivan?" Thea says.

"I don't know. What about the name Park?"

"Park's cute," Thea says. "I can see that. Ivan and Magnolia with their baby, Park." Thea gives us all a wide smile as if her optimism will dissipate the gnawing dread she knows I am carrying. "You know, Park is actually a really solid name; it's pretty adorable."

"It was on the top of the list on the boys' names side," he tells her.

Thea looks over at me. "Were there any other top contenders for a boy's name?"

I can see what they're doing. Trying to make this less unbearable.

"I like Park or Jonah," I say, remembering the list I wrote in a notebook. "I liked that name."

"Well, why don't you just give him your favorite for now, and later you can adjust, if need be," Thea says. "Nothing's permanent, you know."

"You can do the honors," I say to Ivan. "I mean it."

And I do. I need him to do it, actually.

Because I don't want to name this baby. This baby literally has nothing to do with me except, for some unknown reason, I've been temporarily crowned his caregiver.

It's a privilege and an honor, sure, that I get to make sure this brand-new life doesn't end up in a bad situation. I can and will protect him but just as a placeholder.

I'm not his mother.

"Park it is," Ivan says with a grin. He lifts Park, holding him in the crook of his arm. "God, he's adorable. I can't wait till he's big enough for mommy-and-me yoga."

"You mean daddy and me?" Thea asks with a grin.

He chuckles. "True. How about parents-and-me yoga? That's more progressive anyway, right?"

"I think so," Thea says. "And Arden and I would come. It sounds awesome. Even though, right now, he's more interested in throwing blocks than he is stretching."

"Baby steps, right?" Ivan says. "The kid just learned to walk."

It's true, Thea's son has only been walking a short while. I smile, remembering him being a late walker. She'd become anxious about it. It wasn't until a month ago he started making moves across the living room without holding on to a cushion on the couch. Thea had agonized for months that he wasn't hitting his milestones soon enough, but then, just like magic, one day he did. Instead of falling over and crawling everywhere, he stood up straight and moved across the room as if he knew exactly what he was doing.

If the baby in my arm were mine, then these two boys would grow up as close as cousins. But that's not going to happen, because this baby does not belong to me. And I cannot help but feel a growing sense of guilt that this boy — Park — is not with his mother. He deserves that. She deserves that too.

When we get in the car, I sit in the back again with Park. Ivan pauses at the back passenger door before shutting me in. His blue eyes are full of clarity. I can feel his joy as he looks at me. I wish I could match his happiness. But right now, the smiles feel forced, made on command.

"I'm proud of you, babe," he says.

"Proud of me," I repeat with a smirk. "For what? Putting on a brave face for an hour?"

"For doing your best," he says softly. He kisses me softly on the lips, and I sigh, appreciating his tenderness to me. I am sure he is conflicted on so many levels, yet he is giving me nothing but respect at this moment.

"I love you," I tell him, meaning it.

Ivan is the best thing that ever happened to me. He was my rock after I lost my grandma. He was my safety net after I lost Lucy, and now he is my partner waiting out this new storm. At least, I hope he is. If he doesn't stay close, I'm scared I'll blow away. I need him to know that I am his partner, through thick and thin.

In the car on the drive home, Ivan brings up the topic that I'm dreading. "So," he says, "I know you keep fantasizing about a daughter, so you think I should call Dr. Bryerson for another house call?"

"You don't need to do that," I say without pause. The last thing I want is my shrink back at the house.

"But, Mags, if it doesn't stop, I . . ."

"What," I ask, looking down at Park in the infant car seat. He is so angelic, sleeping soundly. "Your threat will be a reality?"

"There's no threat," he says. "It's safety that I'm most concerned about. I don't want anything to happen that could harm you or Park. I just . . ."

Those words cause me to still. "You think I'd hurt this baby?"

"I don't know what to think," he says. "You're hell-bent on this story that everybody knows isn't true and—"

"Fine," I say, resigned to letting him think I will give him what he wants. Even if I know I am going to do anything but. He shouldn't think I am on a mission. "I'll drop it."

He exhales. "Oh, Mags. That is so good to hear. The last thing I want is for you to go back . . ." His words trail off because there is no good way to end this train of thought.

My whole body is frigid, cold like ice, but I don't care. I need to keep my emotions in check even if it means growing tenser.

I'm suddenly feeling so upset with Ivan. Why can't he listen to me and imagine what I am saying might be true? Why is he assuming the absolute worst? Why do they all think I'm crazy, and they are completely sane?

They will all feel so awful when they learn I have been right. But why can't they avoid that by just pausing to listen to me now?

I need to somehow prove that this baby isn't mine. Asking for a paternity test feels out of the question — the entire island would find out somehow, and I would be labeled a freak, forever.

As the silence from Ivan's unfinished sentence hangs in the air, I finally find the words I need to speak. "I wish there was someone who understood me. Who believed me."

"There are plenty of people who understand you. They're called grief support groups," he says, his voice noticeably tight. "And I've been trying to get you to go for a year."

My face flushes with heat, knowing my avoidance of support groups has only amplified the doubt around my mental clarity. If I didn't want to process how we lost Lucy with other people, maybe that means I haven't processed enough. Maybe that is why I am so insistent that I have a daughter now.

"Right," I say. "Of course. I should have gone and sat in a circle and told people about my baby who died. Sounds like a really good healing experience."

"It was for me," Ivan says gently. He never yells or argues. He is a patient man — probably from all his yoga — but right now, it infuriates me. Suddenly the space between us feels much too wide, the way to the other side impossible.

I swallow, remembering that Ivan went to a grief group for the two months when I was in the hospital. And the poor man didn't think he'd just lost his newborn daughter. He also thought he'd lost his wife — maybe forever.

"I'm sorry," I say. "There's nothing against them. I'm just not there right now."

"You don't need to apologize to me," he says.

"What should I do, then?" I ask, feeling frustrated.

"I think you need to focus on doing what your doctor said. Taking care of yourself, taking your meds and reminding yourself of the facts. Park is your baby. Park is your baby. Park is your baby."

His words keep repeating themselves, like a new mantra. Forget *I can do hard things*.

Apparently, *Park is my baby* is the statement I need to have on auto-repeat in my mind. It's one thing to doubt my strength, but isn't it an entirely different thing to doubt this child as my own?

I repeat the mantra anyway because if I go to a mental hospital, then there's no way in hell I'm going to get my daughter back.

*Park is my baby.*

I can say that all day and night if I need to, but while I do, you can sure as hell believe I'm going to be looking for my daughter.

# CHAPTER SIX

The next morning, Ivan and I get loaded back into the car with Park. The ride this time is a little less stressful, and even though I was complaining about Melody, I'm realizing having her at the house is actually a bigger blessing than I expected. She washed the clothes, washed the dishes and rocked the crying baby so I could shower. I even dried my hair. This is not the new motherhood I expected, but it's not including sleepless nights, and that seems like a gift from the heavens I don't deserve.

Ivan takes my hand as I sit in the front seat with him. "Do you want to do the drive-through and get coffee for the ferry?" he asks.

I smile. "Sure, that sounds great." It's an ordinary act of kindness, going to the drive-through of our local coffee stand and getting two twelve-ounce lattes with oat milk. We're nothing if not Pacific Northwesterners.

"So, I was thinking," Ivan begins, "maybe we should see if we could hire someone else to be a longer-term nanny." He says this as he pulls into the ferry dock. The boat has just pulled up, and we're going to load in a few minutes. He puts the car in park.

"Melody probably can't stay forever, I guess, huh?" I say with a little smile.

Ivan nods. "She says Homewood needs her, which makes sense. This was a last-minute godsend, you know?"

I nod. "I'm glad she is here. At first, I wasn't, but it has made everything easier." I sigh.

I look out the window at the Puget Sound before us, the glistening blue waters, the tall cedars. It's a majestic place to live. And every time I pull up to this dock, I'm reminded of how beautiful this island has become to me, how dear it is.

"Where do you even go about finding a nanny?" I ask. I'm being acquiescent to my husband. If hiring a nanny will take the focus off me, I am all for it. The last thing I want is for Ivan to be stressed out and think I will go back to an inpatient hospital.

I'm not going to tell him my plan to find out who has my daughter and bring her home, offering up this baby in return. People don't steal babies without ill intent. Swapping them is even more bizarre. Someone wanted to hurt my family or me. Someone has an agenda I know nothing about. I need answers.

These are the things I'm always thinking about while I'm nursing Park in the middle of the night; this is what is on my mind constantly.

My daughter was taken. Someone wanted her, but why? Why would someone want my little girl and be willing to offer up theirs in return? And besides, how many babies are born on the San Juan Islands? And wouldn't I know nearly every single one of the mothers-to-be?

Though that's not true, at least not this year, since I haven't been working. I don't know anyone, really, besides Thea. I stick to my house. I putter around the yard. I work in my garden. I knit half a dozen baby blankets and sage-green cardigans to fit a three-month-old. That's how I've spent the year.

That and rubbing my belly, praying to God that this baby will be born alive.

So no, I don't know anybody ready to give birth in this month or so. I don't know who would have swapped our babies.

"Mags? Are you okay? I feel like I lost you," Ivan says. He puts the car into drive, pulling us onto the ferry.

"I'm here," I say, smiling over at him. I clutch his hand as it rests on the gearshift. "I am. It's just been a long week."

"Yeah," he says, "it has. But man, Park's cute, right? I swear to God, I melt when I hold him."

"Me too," I say, which is true. Park is literal perfection. A bundle of bliss that I have the privilege of holding.

Maybe it's not my baby I'm bonding to, but I am attached to Park. I am doing my best to nurture and give him what any newborn needs. And he's lucky. It's not just me taking care of him. He has me, Ivan, Melody and maybe soon another nanny. I don't know.

"So where do you go about finding a nanny anyway?" I ask, "Through, like, a website or something?"

"I asked Thea if she had any recommendations," Ivan tells me.

I frown. "You talked to Thea about this?" I'm confused, in all honesty. Why is my husband talking to my best friend about this?

On the other hand, this should be expected. I know everyone on this island is talking about me. My husband and best friend are too.

Besides, maybe Ivan wants to keep this additional burden off my plate. I appreciate that.

"Thanks for taking that on, Ivan," I say. "Did Thea have any leads?"

"Not yet, but she's going to ask around. It sounds like she knows some people in a mommy's group based in the Greater Seattle Area. They are in a Facebook group together."

"Keep me posted," I say, squeezing his hand. "I just have a few requests for a nanny."

"Like what?" Ivan asks me with a warm smile.

"I would prefer someone who isn't super chatty; I like things quiet. And someone who can handle the fact that we don't have a TV."

Ivan smiles. "So demanding."

I laugh. "That's why you love me, right?"

He smiles back. "Something like that."

When we pull up to Homewood, the midwifery clinic, the air is windy, and the sky is covered in clouds. Ivan quickly transfers Park from the car seat to a sling around his torso. I help tuck Park in nice and cozy, then grab the diaper bag. We quickly cross the small parking lot to avoid the rain that threatens to fall.

I'm relieved when I walk in the front doors. It feels familiar. I haven't been here in so long. Most midwife visits are in the client's home.

Hollis has been my midwife and has been doing weekly visits for the last few months. She comes to my home and would have today as well, but I wanted to leave the island and get a change of scenery.

When we enter the clinic, I notice everyone gives Ivan a once-over. I'm not surprised. He looks so handsome and happy with his black beanie on and the baby against his chest. He looks like the quintessential Pacific Northwestern dad, wearing a linen sling and holding the newborn.

I press my lips together, wishing it was our baby in that sling. The thought needs to be replaced, though; I am not looking to pry open a case against me and my mental health. I am looking for information on recent births on the island.

Clover greets me, "Oh my goodness, it's so good to see you, mama." She gives me a great big hug.

The midwifery room smells like sage and eucalyptus, the air diffuser emitting fragrant essential oil aromatherapy. There are linen window coverings, and soft instrumental music is playing through the wall-mounted speakers. A dream catcher, gifted by a client a few years ago, hangs in the window. Next, there's a mural full of photographs of the babies we've helped bring into the world.

I smile, looking at them, thinking how my new daughter's photo should be up there. Before I can finish the thought, though, Clover has joined me at the mural, the Polaroid camera we use to snap these pictures in her hand.

"It's time for a picture of baby Park," she says with a cheerful smile.

I swallow, her words catching me off guard. Park is going up there on the wall.

That's not what I am thinking at all, what I am wanting. He isn't mine to display.

I am thinking . . . does it even matter?

I tell myself to calm down, take a deep breath; having a panic attack right now isn't going to help. Besides, she is just asking for a photograph of this cute, precious baby. The issue is that I have yet to learn to whom he belongs.

While carrying the baby in the sling, Ivan gently positions Park's face toward the camera.

Clover smiles and takes a photograph. After it slides out of the camera, she shakes it in her hand a few times before setting it down on the counter. Looking at us, she smiles.

"Well," she says, "now that we've got that taken care of, I think Hollis will be ready to see you."

Before she can say any more, I hear a woman sobbing in one of the exam rooms.

"Who's that?" I ask, alarmed.

Clover grimaces. "That's Billie Davis."

"Why is she crying?" Ivan asks.

Then I remind him. "That's the mother who lost her newborn son last week, the night of the storm."

Ivan frowns. "The night you had Park?"

My body stiffens, but I nod. I am refusing to become dramatic. It sounds like Billie is the one who needs the emotional support today. "God, she must be heartbroken," I manage to say.

"Yes, she is. Donna is with her right now. Hollis couldn't calm her down. It's just terrible, really. Poor thing. She's so young, and losing her baby is a tragedy." Clover runs a hand over her belly. "I feel embarrassed. Like being here, pregnant, is just too cruel. I feel so awful."

"It's okay," I say, looking at Park. "I'm here with a baby too."

"And thank goodness for that, right?" Clover sighs.

"What does Billie need?" I ask.

"Something she can't have. She wants to see the baby. She doesn't believe he's dead. We tried to explain that the baby's not here, that he's at the morgue, but she's not listening."

"Does she have someone you can call?"

"We've been trying the baby's father, Hudson Malone. He's a fisherman, but he comes and leaves. He's on and off again anyway."

"Does she have anybody?" I asked.

Clover shrugs. "I don't know. That's what Hollis is trying to find out. I should be grateful, I think. I have a baby that's alive; Billie doesn't."

Hollis comes out to find me. "Hey," she says. "Look at you. You look so good."

"I feel good," I say, meaning it. "Although I told you I didn't want Melody to come to stay at the house, I think I have been proven wrong. She's incredible. And Ivan is even trying to find a full-time nanny to help for a while to make sure we settle in okay."

"That's wonderful," Hollis says. "You're lucky to have a man like him around, helping you out."

"I know," I say. "He is so happy to be in dad mode."

"Well, are you ready to do an exam on the baby?" she asks. "And Mama too."

"Sure," I say. "Though I know the drill; I've assessed everything. I think everything's pretty good, in working order."

Hollis laughs. "I'm sure it is, but all the same, I have to do due diligence, right?"

"Of course," I say.

Ivan and I follow her into one of the practitioner rooms. He unwraps Park from the sling and hands him to Hollis. "Oh, he looks so happy and healthy. And he hasn't been overly fussy or anything, giving you pretty simple cues when he needs to eat and get changed, that sort of thing?"

"Yeah," I say. "Do you agree, Ivan?" I ask my husband, and he nods. "He nurses every few hours. He likes to sleep, swaddled tight," I say.

Hollis smiles at me, resting a hand on my shoulder. "Oh, Magnolia, it's so good to hear all this. I've been so worried about you."

"Don't worry about me," I say. "I'm a big girl."

"I know, but . . ."

"But nothing," I say. "I can do this. I'm not incapable of being a mother."

"Nobody said you were," Hollis says in a singsong voice, soothing both Park and me.

She lays Park down on an infant-sized mattress pad on the table in the room. "So," she says, "nothing to be concerned about?" She looks Park over. And for the first time, I recognize the birthmark on his right leg, the size of a quarter, brown. How did I not notice that before? Have I been in such a fog?

I want to say something. I want to say that's not my baby because my baby didn't have a birthmark, but I don't know how to put it into words without sounding like a lunatic.

I can't not say something. "Did you notice this before?" I ask. "The birthmark?"

"Yeah, it was there when I did his exam the day after he was born, Mags."

"Right," I say, flustered. "I hadn't noticed. I must be more tired than I thought."

Hollis looks over at Ivan. "Get this girl to sleep when you get home, okay?"

"Of course," Ivan says. "She was with Thea the other day, and this today, maybe it's too much."

"It's not too much," I say. "I'm fine. Everything is fine. It has to be, right?" I say tightly.

Hollis and Ivan give each other a look, that knowing look, the look that says she's not as well as she wants us to believe.

These two know me better than I know myself, it seems. They remember things about those months after Lucy died that I've locked up, hidden away with a key I've thrown into the sea.

Ivan cradles Park in his arm, and together, they leave the room. Hollis gives me a quick exam, confirming what I already know; everything is as it should be.

"Everything okay, Magnolia? I wanted to ask, now that Ivan isn't with us."

"I'm fine," I bristle, redressing. "Why wouldn't I be?"

Hollis shrugs. "I want you to be happy. I'm not trying to make this more difficult, but . . ."

"There are no buts, okay? I am happy and think you're right about me getting some help. We will hire a nanny. I'll rest as much as I can. I'll do what I can to be a good mama to this boy. All right? Everyone happy?" I look at my friend, wanting her to understand I am not going to throw my life away to mess it all up. I have a goal. I have a mission. A mission they don't recognize, but it's mine nonetheless.

"Okay," she relents. "Keep me in the loop if anything changes for you, okay? It would be best if you didn't go back to the place you were after Lucy. No one does."

"I don't want that either." Not wanting to go down this road with her before I have some clue to go on regarding my missing baby, I change the course of the conversation. "Is Billie going to be okay?" I ask Hollis. "I didn't realize she lost a baby the night I had mine."

"She'll be all right," Hollis says. "She's young. She doesn't have any family, but her boss, Tori Bingham, the owner of Swept Away Coffee, is coming to get her right now. Billie won't stop crying. Tori will help her out and make sure she's all right. Tori is the only real support person that Billie has right now."

"That makes me feel like crap," I admit. "Considering I had so many people in my corner after Lucy."

Hollis sighs. "You can't compare. Everyone's circumstances are all so different."

"I'm glad Tori can be there for her," I say. "The last thing she needs is to be on her own."

"You do know that better than anybody, don't you?" Hollis says softly as she opens the door, letting Ivan back in.

Ivan pulls Park back into the sling, and Hollis gives me a long, warm hug goodbye.

I see Tori Bingham pulling up as we leave the clinic. She looks tired. It's a look I recognize. It was the face that Ivan wore after Lucy died. A glimpse of pure exhaustion because it's hard to be someone's everything.

And Ivan was my partner, my husband.

Tori owes Billie nothing.

"I bet she's a mess," I say.

Ivan nods. "I think they're going to be okay. We're all going to be okay." He grips my hand tight, and I squeeze it back.

God, I want to believe him.

# CHAPTER SEVEN

The following day, I feel like I will lose my mind if I keep spinning in circles all on my own, without any more information about the night of the birth.

I need answers, some concrete evidence I can walk forward with, because this path I'm treading, it's one of madness. If this baby boy, Park, isn't my child, which I know in my gut he is not, that means my baby's somewhere else and that someone has to have seen something.

While Melody rocks Park to sleep in the living room, I take a moment to dry my hair, then put on clean leggings and a pair of galoshes. The fields outside my house are wet, so I need waterproof shoes for this hike.

In the living room, Ivan looks up from the floor. He's in a bow pose, legs and arms spread behind him — his eyes to the sky.

"Hey," he says.

On the yoga mat, he looks so vulnerable, so different than he usually is. Always is. In day-to-day life, he's a rock. My rock.

He lets go of his ankles and uses his palms to push himself off the floor.

"Where are you headed?" he asks.

"I'm going to take a walk outside," I say.

"Want company?"

I shake my head. "No, I just want to be alone for a bit." He watches me but doesn't comment. In the kitchen, I pour myself a to-go cup of coffee. "Are you okay with the baby? I need some fresh air to clear my head."

"Of course," he says. "Anything you need, everything you need. We got you." He looks over at Melody, and they share a smile. "Right?"

She nods. "Of course, Park isn't that difficult to take care of. Look at this guy. He is so cute."

I smile in agreement. He may not be my baby, but he is adorable.

"I won't be long," I say. "I just want to go down to the end of the street and back."

"Whatever you want," he says.

Outside, I breathe in the fresh air of the island. Even though it's been a windy week, the sky has begun to part and reveal stretches of blue. The late-morning sun hangs in the sky and fills my face with a warmth I didn't realize I needed.

Sleep, while not soundless, has still been pretty easy coming, considering I just gave birth. Would it be easier or more complicated if it were my baby I was rocking to sleep? If it would be harder to let her go, to take a break, a walk. Deciding there's no point in dwelling on the what-ifs, I just put one foot in front of the other, taking a sip of my coffee as I go. I have a destination in mind. I didn't explain that to Ivan. The last thing I wanted was to ring any alarm bells, but I know. I need something to go off of, and my neighbor Rooney is the only one who can give it to me.

His house shares a driveway with mine. When I get there, the curtains are pulled, but he's out on the front porch puttering around with a pipe in his mouth. I smile as I greet him.

"Hey," he says. "Look at you, Magnolia! I heard you had a baby."

I smile. "You heard that already, huh?"

"Small island," he says. "Everybody talks."

"I wasn't sure you were leaving your house much these days," I tease.

I sit next to him on the front porch, and he puffs on his pipe.

"You don't mind, do you?"

I shake my head. "Not when we're outside."

He smiles at me. "So where's this baby? I thought you were going to come to show him off."

"Oh, he's sleeping with Ivan, and I just wanted some fresh air. Maybe some company."

Rooney gives me a wink. "Aw, you're an angel, Mags. What do you have to do with some older man? You must be lonely up in your house if you want my company."

"Not lonely," I say. "I feel cooped up. I wanted to get outside and stretch my legs. It was a pretty wild night when I gave birth," I say.

He nods slowly. "It sure was a wild storm, that's for certain. And I heard you gave birth all on your own. Other women might not have fared so well if they hadn't had the training you had. Your boy's lucky, Maggie. Very lucky."

I nod. "I know. It could have been so much worse. Somehow fortune favored us."

He nods. "It sure does."

"I was wondering," I say, "before Ivan came home, was anyone else on the road that night? Our road. I'd been so busy giving birth but swore I heard a car."

I chose my words carefully, hoping they could lead him to where I wanted him to go. Of course, I didn't hear a car — but I can't say that. I need him to tell me if he saw a car.

Rooney's recollection of the night spills quickly. "Actually," he says, "there were two cars down your driveway that night."

"Two," I say. "Not Ivan's?"

He shakes his head. "No. Well, one was a silver four-door car, and one was a tiny Ford Focus."

"A Ford Focus," I say.

He nods. "Yeah."

"Right," I say. "Did you see people in the cars?"

"I wasn't paying that much attention. I just heard the noise. I'd been watching out the window for the storm. I have my generator, you know, so I didn't lose power."

"Interesting," I say, shaking my head. "I don't know why we haven't gotten one of those yet."

"I know. You'll have to now," he says. "You're a parent. You've got to make sure you protect yourself and your little guy."

"I agree. Maybe Ivan can get us one," I say. "So these cars just came and went?"

He shrugs. "Hard to say, Magnolia. I wasn't paying too much attention to them; I was more concerned with the weather. I don't know what you want me to tell you."

"It's okay," I say. "Doesn't matter. No one seemed to come over that night. Not until Ivan got home, and I was sound asleep when he did."

Park nods and smiles at me. "All right, so tell me, when will you bring your son over here? Let me meet him."

I smile at him. "You like babies?" For some reason, he doesn't strike me as the kind of man who would.

He chuckles. "Of course, who wouldn't love a wrin-kled-up gremlin?"

"Do you have kids, Rooney? I've never seen kids over here."

"I had a boy."

"Had?" I ask.

He nods slowly. "Yeah, but he died when he was thir-ty-five. Heartbreak, right? Overdose. Never saw it coming."

"I'm so sorry," I say.

"I know you've had your fair share of loss. I never brought it up before because the loss of a baby differs from the loss of a grown man."

"Maybe your loss is worse than mine."

"That's not how grief works, Magnolia."

"It isn't?" I say.

He shakes his head, pulling the flask from his pocket. He takes a long sip. He offers it to me, and I take it from

60

his hands. I unscrew the cap of my coffee cup, and I pour in some of the whiskey.

He smiles. "There you go. Good mama." I laugh. He continues. "The thing about grief is, and loss is, there's not a competition for who has it worse. It sucks all the same. Sucks the life out of you. The joy is out of you as long as you let it. I'm happy you had another shot at being a mom. Now you have a healthy child," he says, nodding firmly. "And that means you're giving yourself a chance to move on, to love again."

"You never got that chance, huh?"

He shakes his head. "No, I'm an old man. You know that. And honestly, I was just happy about my time with Luke."

"That was his name?" I say.

He nods. "Yeah. What did you name your boy?"

"Ivan named him Park," I tell him.

Rooney smiles. "Well, there's a good name you don't hear too often."

"Luke is a solid name too," I say. "No one messes with a Luke."

He laughs. "May be true. But losing him? It did mess with my mind a bit."

"Well, I can relate to that," I say softly. I take a sip of my coffee. "Thanks for being the lookout of our street. Especially now that I have a baby at home, and Ivan travels a lot, it feels good knowing that someone else is watching out for me."

"I am," he says. "I'll always have your back, Magnolia."

I smile. "Thanks." I stand and walk off the porch. I lift my coffee cup toward him. "Thanks for the booze."

"Well, you know I'm always good for that," he says with a chuckle.

I walk away, back to my home, thinking about what he said. Not just about loss, grief and holes that are filled and emptied — but also the cars.

Hollis drives a black Ford Focus. But I already knew she was coming to my home that following day.

But there was someone else. Someone in a silver four-door sedan.

Who?

I don't know. My heart aches, terrified. Because what if the owner of that car is the person who has my baby?

# CHAPTER EIGHT

When I return to the house, I feel a growing sense of frustration. I know this baby isn't mine, and a silver car was down my driveway. Beyond that — I feel lost.

Melody senses something's up. "Hey," she says. "You look upset? Something happen?"

I shake my head. "Why would you think something happened?"

Her eyes widen, handing me Park, who's just begun to fuss. "Sorry," she says, "I wasn't trying to . . ."

"What? Why would something bad happen to me? What are you trying to say?"

"I'm not starting anything," she says. "I think Park's hungry." She walks away without another word, but I notice her eyes catching on Ivan's again.

He walks toward me with trepidation.

"What?" I ask. "You don't have to walk on eggshells around me. I'm fine."

"You don't seem fine. You seem a little tense."

"Right. Crazy thing, right? I was slightly tense after I just gave birth a few days ago. You have Melody babysitting me in my house, and you don't think I'd be tense?"

"Hey," he says. "Mags, where's this coming from?"

"Where's it coming from? Where *isn't* it coming from?" I sit on the couch, unhooking my nursing bra. Park squeals in my arms, and I want to make him stop crying, make him happy — but I also wish I were his mother. Tears fill my eyes, frustration gnawing at me. Ivan looks at me like I have jumped ship.

I swear I can feel him itching to reach into his pocket and grab his phone to call an emergency meeting with Dr. Bryerson, find an opportunity to get me in a car and send me off to a psych ward.

*I've got to keep it together.*

I rock Park as he takes my breast. My milk has come in fully, and there's a relief as he suckles against me. I sigh at the sensation. It's so wholly unexpected.

"Are you okay?" Ivan asks.

"It's just a lot, like there's a baby on top of me, like literally on top of me, and you're looking at me like that. And Melody's hovering, and . . ."

"Nobody is hovering. Nobody is doing anything," he says. "God, I thought the walk would do you some good, but you're just as spun-up as ever."

"I'm not spun-up. I'm just trying to process."

Ivan sits down on the couch next to me. "Motherhood is complicated. I can't pretend to know that, but I'm a new father too. I'm figuring this out just the same as you."

I bite back a laugh. "Right, just the same," I say. "Totally the same."

He frowns. "I don't know what you want from me. I'm trying to support you, take care of you, but . . ."

"And I appreciate that," I say. "It's just . . ."

"What?" he asks.

"It's a lot to deal with."

"Do you want me to call Hollis, see if she can come over, or Thea?"

I latch on to that. "Yes, Thea. Maybe I can meet her in town for coffee."

"You up for that?" he asks. "You're not too worn out?"

"No," I say. "I'm fine. At least, I think I am."

"You want to take Park with you?" he asks. "It'd be your first trip in the car by yourself."

I think about that. "Maybe you could drive me?" I recognize my limits . . . my capacity.

He nods. "All right. Why don't you call Thea and see when she's available today? I've got nothing going on this afternoon."

"When do you go back to work?" I ask.

"I took all of the next month off, thinking that's when you'd have the baby. I canceled the few workshops I was having over the next few weeks, so you've got me for six weeks, babe. I'm not going anywhere. I'll be your chauffeur, a personal chef and a dog walker."

"We don't have a dog."

He grins. "Right, but if we did, I'd be at its beck and call."

"I don't need you to wait on me, hand and foot," I say.

"I know," he says with a smile. "You're a progressive woman who can handle all sorts of things. However, as your husband and this boy's father, I wouldn't mind doing my fair share. After all, you're the one who carried him in your womb for nine months. What did I do, besides knocking you up?" He kisses me on the cheek.

Leaning back against the sofa as he walks out of the room, I try to take a deep breath, realizing that getting wound up, like I just did, isn't going to help the situation.

I need to find that silver car. With that thought, I text Thea.

*Hey, want to meet up for a walk downtown and get coffee?*

She replies immediately.

*Perfect. When Tanner's home, and he gets off early today, around three. Sound good? In front of Top of the Morning?*

I reply with a thumbs-up and then fill Ivan in on the plans.

"Perfect. So we'll get ready to go in a few hours. After lunch, we'll head downtown. Sound good?"

"Yes," I say with the first smile of my day. "Now stop hovering. Let me be my own person."

Later in the afternoon, Ivan, Park, and I head downtown. Ivan helps me adjust the sling against my body this time, both of us laughing as we carefully place Park inside the cocoon.

When I see Thea, I immediately feel more relaxed. It's not that Ivan stresses me out; it's just that Thea isn't threatening me with a stay at the psych ward.

"Hey, baby," she says, heading straight for Park, ignoring me.

"Okay, is this how it goes?" I ask with a laugh. "Mothers become chopped liver the moment they give birth?"

"Basically," she says dryly. "Hey, Ivan. How's it going? How are you doing with being a new dad?"

He shrugs. "Pretty good. Did you find any leads for nannies on your message board?"

"Actually, I did," she says. "I was going to text them to you, but I just wanted to make sure you were still interested before I hit send."

"We're both interested," I say, speaking for Ivan. I want him to know that I am fully supportive of getting help, of securing resources, especially the ones he wants. I don't want to give him any reason for alarm.

Thea pulls her phone from her purse and copies and pastes something before pressing send.

A moment later, Ivan smiles. "Got it," he says, "Actually, I'm going to go inside this coffee shop while you guys take your walk and follow up on some of these leads."

"Thanks, honey," I say, kissing him.

A few minutes later, coffees in hand, Thea and I begin walking the small downtown street.

"So you want a nanny?" Thea asks.

Park is tight against my chest, and I breathe in the fresh island air, feeling alive. "I mean, I'm fine with the idea; I know I am not entirely stable after the last year. But if someone is going to be living with us, I'd rather have someone not connected to our life."

"Melody is already annoying?" she asks.

"I mean, she's a nice enough girl, but it's kind of weird how she knows so much about Ivan and me."

"Ooh, what's the hot gossip on you and Ivan?"

I laugh. "There's nothing hot, you know that. We're a boring married couple who have barely gotten ourselves this far."

"Hey," she says. "You and Ivan are great together."

"I know," I say, "and I'm grateful for him; it's just been a hell of a year. Hell of a *few* years."

"I know, Maggie," she says, wrapping an arm around my shoulder and resting her head against it. "I got your back," she says. "Always. And maybe there'll be some nice nanny who won't bug you so much. Having an old coworker inside my house would drive me batty."

"So, anything going on with you and your family?" I ask her.

She shrugs. "The usual. Arden and I have been going to that mommy-and-me class over on Orcas, once a week. He loves it. Me, not so much. I don't really know how I'm supposed to make friends with other moms. It's like they're more into it than I am or know how to do it better than me."

"Thea." I laugh. "you're an amazing mother."

"You think?" she says. "Most of the time, I feel like I'm messing up. God, I mentioned trying to sleep-train Arden, and you should have seen the looks I got."

"To each their own, right?"

"Well, that's what I tell myself," she says, "but then I'm sitting in the mommy group, and these women look at me like I'm a child abuser."

"Thea," I say with a laugh, "you're not a child abuser." Dropping my tone, I add, "You're a mom who's surviving, thriving."

"And you?" she says, "How are you guys doing?"

I bring Park's head to my lips, kissing him. "We're fine," I say, leaving it at that.

As we walk, I notice a silver four-door car parked outside the local pizza shop. "Whose car is that?" I ask.

Thea gives me a strange look. "I don't know all the cars on this island."

"Well, only two hundred people live here; it's not hard to know whose car is whose."

"Sure, but . . ."

"You don't know either?"

"You can ask them," she says as a couple exits the pizzeria with a key fob in their hand. They unlock the door and move to open it.

"Excuse me," I say, getting their attention.

"Do I know you?" the woman asks.

"No, I was just wondering how long you've been in town."

The woman gives me a strange look. "We're staying here about a week on vacation. Maybe a little more, depending on whether we can convince the Airbnb that we are great long-term renters."

I frown. "An Airbnb?"

"Yeah," she says. "You live on the island?"

"Yeah, I do. I live over on Harris Drive."

"Harris Drive," she says slowly. "That's so random. That's the street close to where we're staying."

"Really?"

Thea looks between us. "I feel like I'm missing something," she says. "Hi, I'm Thea." She sticks out her hand to the woman.

"I'm Nancy," she says. "This is my husband, Rob."

"Hey, guys," he says.

"Hi, I'm Magnolia, and this is Park. We live on Harris Drive, and anyway, this sounds a little crazy, but do you happen to know if you were driving down that street the night of the wild rainstorm?"

"Oh my God, were we ever." Rob chuckles. "That was our first night here, and we took that street, and we didn't know where we were going. I was going to lose my mind because there was no cell service. The power was out everywhere; it was pitch dark."

"Bad night to get on a new island," Thea says.

"You're telling me," Rob replies. "So you live over on Harris Drive?" he asks.

I nod. "Yeah, there's only a few houses on that road," I tell him.

"We noticed," the woman says. "But we're staying over on Montgomery. It's just one road over. We took a left turn too soon."

"Right," I say, looking her over.

She's a little standoffish, a little cool, and a little calculating in how she looks me up and down as if wondering what I'm up to.

If she only knew.

"Anyway," I say, "nice to meet you, and now you know a neighbor, if you end up being a long-term renter."

"Right," she says. "If we do." She frowns, turning to her husband. "Should we go?" To Thea and me, she points to the box in her hand. "We just got pizza."

"Right," I say. "Enjoy."

They leave, pulling away in the car, and Thea looks at me like I'm crazy. "What was that about? Since when do you go up to people, asking them if they've ever been on your street before?"

I press my lips together. "Do you really want to know the answer to that?" I ask her.

She raises her eyes. "Yeah, I'm your best friend. Of course I do."

"Rooney told me two cars were on my road the night of the storm. One of them was Hollis's Ford Focus, and the other was a four-door silver car. And that night, somebody took my baby."

69

Thea pulls in a breath. "And you think these vacationers are also baby swappers?"

"I don't know what to think," I tell her, "but I know somebody knows something. I need to find out who that somebody is."

# CHAPTER NINE

After Park is nursed and swaddled for the night, I take a long, hot shower. My goal is to clear my head and think things through. Right now, I feel like I am on the edge of reason, the edge of everything.

Hollis texts, checking in on me, and I tell her things are fine. She asks if I've talked to Dr. Bryerson again, and I tell her I haven't: *Everything is going just fine.* If I say it often enough, it might become true, right?

Maybe I say fine one too many times because the last thing she texts me before I set my phone down is:

*If you want to talk, I'm always here for you. You don't have to hide things from me. We've been friends for far too long for that.*

There's a pang of guilt gnawing inside of me. Not because I want to hide anything from someone who I know cares deeply about my family and me, but because it feels strange to think she's wrong, that Ivan and Thea — everybody — is seeing things so differently than I am. *Maybe I am crazy.*

I get dressed in yoga pants and a sweatshirt and then comb my hair before braiding it. In the kitchen, I make myself a mug of chamomile tea. Melody slept in the guest room a few hours ago, and Ivan is practicing meditation in the living room. He'll hear Park if he wakes, allowing me to slip outside.

I grab a flashlight in the mudroom and pull on a thick, heavy coat. Then I make my way across the yard, not telling anybody I'm leaving. It's not that I want to go in secret, but I know anything I say or do will be held against me by my husband and my psychiatrist. It's better to ask for forgiveness than permission because the alternative to being caught snooping around an Airbnb one road over is me ending up at the psych ward, my daughter not found.

The air is crisp and cool. The sky is black. I breathe it in, the trees and the wind and the waves. I love this place, this island. It feels like home. The conversation Thea and I had over a year ago, when we were both pregnant for the first time, wanting to raise our children in a place like this, hasn't changed much for me. I love the sanctuary of these vast open spaces.

I close my eyes, trying to center myself, trying not to get lost in my head, but I wonder if I have gotten lost out here on this island. Maybe being at the house all day, every day, for the last year during my leave of absence has caused me to spiral in ways I hadn't realized.

Maybe I've gone mad. Perhaps I've just been hiding it.

My mind is a mess — Park is so beautiful, so sweet and adorably cute. I want him to be happy and healthy, yet I feel nothing maternal toward him. Maybe I'm just not very attached as a mother. Perhaps I put too much emphasis on the whole thing for so long, and now that it's here, I don't know what a good thing it is.

Maybe I was delusional the night I gave birth. Or I was clinging to repressed memories, and I imposed them upon Park.

Tears fill my eyes at this thought because it makes me feel like a monster. Like I'm messing everything up. Maybe I already have. This is not what I thought motherhood would be. It's only been five days, but I feel swept away by the current. Like I'll never be able to keep treading this water. Like I'll drown.

I cross Harris Drive through our backyard and cut down Montgomery Avenue. Flashing my light, I can locate the four-door silver sedan. It's parked in front of a small cottage, which is painted white with green shutters and a giant cedar tree in the front yard. There's a small window on the porch. Not wanting to creep toward the light, I edge away toward the side of the house, where I discover a bigger window. I turn off the flashlight, guided by the light of the cottage.

From the living room window, I can see the man and woman, Nancy and Rob, whom I met earlier. They're picking up wineglasses off the kitchen counter and carrying them down the hall.

I watch them, knowing I'm spying. Knowing this is more than a little creepy but also desperate for insight. It would've been easier if I had seen them holding a baby, rocking one to sleep. I was hoping to see a pack-and-play or a swing set up in this living room, but there's nothing suspicious.

I need something concrete.

Walking closer to the window, I crouch now that they're gone, probably to a bedroom to have one glass of wine before they fall asleep.

Looking through the window, I scan the room. It's pretty standard Ikea furniture. A couch and table, glasses and plates on open shelving in the kitchen. But when I glance down at the kitchen counter next to a corked bottle of wine, I see something else.

Something that makes my blood go cold.

My heart begins to pound. I must be seeing things.

I blink and I blink. But no, it's there.

A pacifier sits on the kitchen counter. Panicked, I look again for any signs of an infant: a car seat, something. Before I can continue staring into this space that is not mine, I see Nancy walking out of the hallway, laughing. She reaches for a book on the coffee table in the living room.

I dip my head down low, scared to be caught.

Terrified of Nancy seeing me, I decide not to risk it. Getting caught spying would be a huge red flag to Ivan. I can't be found out. I count to ten before crawling along the ground toward my yard on Harris Drive.

When I enter the cabin, fifteen minutes have passed. Ivan is still in the middle of his meditation, oblivious. Melody hasn't opened her door, and Park is still sound asleep. I let out a shaky breath, wondering what to do next.

In the mudroom, I take off my boots and coat, hang the flashlight on a hook and press my hands to my chest.

I saw that, didn't I? I'm not making this up.

I don't know how to explain this to Ivan without him thinking I've lost it. But I have to say something, don't I?

Before I can broach the subject or figure out how to do that, Ivan has snapped out of his meditation and finds me in the mudroom.

"Hey," he says. "What are you doing back here?"

"Sorry, I didn't want to bug you. I thought you were still meditating, and I was going to step outside for some fresh air."

"Do you want company?" he asks.

I press my lips together. "Actually, maybe I don't want to go outside," I say. "Melody needs to sleep. Maybe we could hang out in the living room until Park wakes."

"Want me to pour you a glass of wine? Make you a cocktail?"

I look at my husband, wanting him to be on my side. Scared if I say much more, he's not going to be. I need to win him over.

I smile. "Do you think you could make us old-fashioneds?"

He grins. "Those are my specialties."

"Look at us," I say. "New parents, casually having cock-tails. It's like we're old hat at this."

He laughs, pulling me to him, wrapping his arms around my waist, and tilting my chin ever so slightly before giving me a kiss that's tender, sweet, and filled with the promise of forever.

74

He looks into my eyes. "I love you, Mags."

"I love you, too, Ivan," I tell him.

And I do. I love him more . . . more than . . . The words catch in my mind — more than Park.

That's not right, however. You can't love your husband more than your child. The hierarchy shifts, doesn't it, after you give birth? It should, at least.

"What?" he asks, as if able to tell my thoughts are swirling.

At least reading that, I'm thinking something that's not about a kiss.

"Nothing," I say. "Thank you," I add, "for taking such good care of me."

"I always will," he says. "I'll always take care of you and Park."

I wrap my arms around him tight, snug around his neck, and I breathe him in and kiss his skin.

"Forget the cocktail," I say. "Let's make out."

## CHAPTER TEN

In the morning, I'm greeted by sunshine streaming through my bedroom window, Park snuggled in my arms, Ivan next to me, still sleeping. I take a long, deep breath, savoring this sweet moment.

Ivan and I needed it last night. We needed to kiss and touch and hold. My body is still so tender from giving birth, but I needed my husband to wrap his arms around me and kiss my shoulders and my neck and remind me that I am beautiful and that I am his, and for a moment, it felt as if I had not lost my goddamned mind.

Instead, I felt loved, plain and simple. I wanted him to feel loved too. Not because I'm trying to convince him of something, even though I am, but because I do love Ivan. I want him to know I am more than this woman hell-bent on finding her daughter. I want him to know I am real and living and breathing. His.

He must feel me watching him because he wakes, his eyes blinking sleepily as he takes in this picture. "Wow," he says. "I've waited all my life to see you lying in bed with our baby in your arms." He leans over and kisses me, and I kiss him back, and at the motion, Park squirms.

I smile at this sweet pea, offering him my breast before closing my eyes again. "I slept so hard last night," I tell him.

"Me too," he says. "A few times, Park woke. He calmed right back down. I guess you have a mother's touch."

I smile. "Maybe we don't need a nanny after all?"

He tenses at that. "Okay, well, one thing at a time, all right? You sure you're doing good?"

I nod. "Last night was good."

"Yeah," he says, rolling out of bed. "It was perfect. I've missed you, Magnolia. For so long."

"I know," I say softly, "I was pregnant for two years straight, right?"

He nods. "I wasn't saying that."

"But you were thinking it?"

He shrugs. "Maybe a little. I miss being close to you."

"In time, I'll heal, and we can be close again. I want that more than you know."

"I love this mood of yours," he says with a grin. "How about I make us some coffee while I keep that thought in my mind."

I smile, then laugh at him. "Thank you. Caffeine sounds delicious. And yes, let's hold tight to these sweet memories for as long as possible."

"I love you, you know."

"I love you more," I tell him, meaning it.

A few minutes later, he brings me coffee in bed. I drink from the blue ceramic mug he got me at Christmas, and he takes Park from my arms, burping him, then changing him, redressing him, swaddling him and setting him down in the bassinet.

He tells me Melody is out for a jog. "Maybe it's time she goes home," I suggest.

"You don't like having her here? It's pretty good help. We have all the laundry done and the dishes."

"How much are we paying her?" I ask.

"It doesn't matter. We can afford it."

I twist my lips, wondering if that's true. "I haven't been working for a year."

"Please," he says, "don't go there. Let's enjoy this day. What do you want to do? Anything on your mind? We could binge a TV show on your laptop or do some restorative yoga poses. Both?"

"How about we go for a walk?"

He scrunches his face. "What's up with you and these walks?"

"What?" I say. "I love walking."

"I know, but where are you wanting to go?"

Cautiously, I set my coffee mug on the side table by my bed, biting my lip. "The thing is . . ." I tell him. "I think . . ." I swallow. "The thing is, there was a car on our road the night I gave birth. It came down the driveway."

"That makes sense. I came home," he says.

"No," I say. "Rooney told me there was another vehicle. A four-door silver car."

Frowning, he sits on the bed next to me. "What are you getting at?"

I explain to him what Rooney said about the couple I saw at the downtown pizza shop. I go so far as to admit to what I was doing last night.

"You were sneaking out of the house and spying on people here on vacation? Damn, Mags, that sounds . . ."

"I know. That sounds crazy. But, Ivan, there was a pacifier on the counter. There's a baby there. Maybe it's our baby."

"That's a massive maybe," he says, "and the problem with that thinking, Magnolia, is that Park is our actual baby." He points at the infant between us.

"Don't get mad at me," I say. "I'm trying to be honest. I'm trying to process."

"I wonder what Dr. Bryerson would think about this."

"I don't care what Dr. Bryerson would think," I say, frustrated. "I care what I think, what I know, and I know something's wrong. I know this boy is not mine." My voice is getting loud, my words taut, and I don't want to cry. I want to keep myself collected. Cool.

I want to stay home. I don't wish to be in the psych ward.

"Ivan . . ." My voice is shallow, soft.

It feels like he's reading my mind, watching everything I'm doing, calculating it, itching to call the doctor.

"Don't," I say. "Don't call the doctor. Just go on a walk with me and see."

"You've lost your grip, Magnolia."

"I know," I say, "and so what? So indulge me for another hour, and then I'll let it go. If it's not this car, then . . ."

"Then what?" he says. "You're just going to move on? You need a new therapist to work you through this new trauma because Dr. Bryerson didn't support you quite well enough to get you through the last."

"It's not my fault Lucy died."

"Nobody said it was. Nobody ever said it was. It was horrible, Mags. I know it was. I was there for all of it." Now he's upset, tears in his eyes, and Park's crying, and Melody's in our bedroom. Her hair's sweaty. She's back from her run in jogging pants and a rain jacket.

"Is everything okay?" she asks. "I just got back and heard—"

"It's fine," I say tightly. "I think maybe . . . maybe you should go."

She looks over at Ivan. "You want me to go?"

He throws his hands up. "I don't know what I want. I want something to be easy for once. For one single day, can we have some peace? Maggie, you're making everybody crazy."

That word is the final straw. I get out of bed, walk to my dresser and pull out clothes. "Fine. If you're not going to talk to Rob and Nancy, then I'll talk to them myself."

"You know their names?" he asks, incredulous.

"Yes, I met them when I was with Thea yesterday. Why do you think I wanted to go downtown? I needed to find this car, and I did because I'm looking for our baby."

Ivan and Melody pause. They look at each other. A look I know all too well, a look that says *This is it. This is when Magnolia steps up to the cliff's edge.*

I dress right in front of them. I don't care anymore. My body is already sagging and bulging and sore. I'm still bleeding. My nipples are cracked. "Park's not mine. I need to find her," I say, not caring how I sound if my words are a whisper, a crack, or a gong. "And that's what I'm going to do."

I finish putting on my clothes, my sneakers laced. I pull on a sweatshirt and walk out the front door.

Ivan follows me a few minutes later, calling for me. "Stop," he says. "Please, just stop."

"Why?" I say. I turn to him, acquiescing. "Why'd you come after me?"

"Because I don't want you to do this part alone. I don't want you to do any of this alone."

Tears fill my eyes, "You think *I* do?"

"I think," he says, pressing his hands on my shoulder, "that everything in life can get confusing sometimes, and right now, it's very confusing for you. But come on, let's meet Rob and Nancy and find out why there's a pacifier on their counter. Right now, I think the best course of action is to have a concrete answer, don't you?"

I nod, pressing my lips together, taking his hand, and lacing my fingers through his.

"Thank you," I say, "for just trying."

My hopes begin to grow the closer we get to their home, and by the time Ivan steps onto the front porch and knocks, I feel a swell of anticipation.

She has to be here, hasn't she?

Rob pulls open the door. "Hey," he says. "Can I help you?" He looks past Ivan and sees me. "Hey, did we meet yesterday?" he asks.

I nod. "Yeah, I'm Magnolia. I live over on Harris Drive."

"Right," he says. Nancy joins us on the porch.

"Hi," she says cautiously.

I remember that coolness from yesterday too. She wasn't exactly glowing to meet me. Outside the pizza parlor, I thought she was shy, but now I'm wondering if she has a secret.

"Can we help you?" she asks.

"Yes," Ivan says, "actually, you can. My wife was on a walk yesterday and glanced through your window."

Nancy frowns. "You were looking in our window?" She looks at her husband. "Should I call someone?"

Ivan shakes his head. "No, seriously, everything's fine. Magnolia's been a little confused lately and wanted to ask you a few things. Could you talk to us briefly and help clear things up?"

"Okay," Rob says slowly. "What do you need help with?"

"I saw a pacifier," I say, my words spilling, "on your kitchen counter, and I didn't know why you had that. You didn't tell me you had a baby, and I don't see you with a baby now, and . . ."

Nancy frowns. "A baby? No, we don't have a baby," she says.

"Then why do you have the pacifier just sitting on the kitchen counter? I saw it last night, next to the wine. You . . ."

At that, they both recoil. "You were watching us last night?" Rob wraps an arm around his wife. "Look," he says. "We're having a few days of vacation. We just sent our youngest off to college, and we wanted a getaway. We don't want any trouble. Not with you, not with anything, but . . ." he says, pausing, looking at Ivan as if he's determined I'm a fragile woman, "there *was* a pacifier here when we arrived. I found it underneath the kitchen counter when I was sweeping yesterday. I set it on the counter in case the people who stayed here before found it. It felt weird to throw it away. But it's not ours. If you want to come in the house and see if there's a baby here, you're more than welcome to."

Ivan shakes his head. "No, we don't need to do that."

"Actually," I say, "we do."

My husband looks at me as if I have not only just stepped up to the cliff but have gone completely over the edge. He'd be right. I will do what it takes to find my daughter.

Rob pulls open the door, and Nancy steps back onto the porch. I walk into the cottage. It's two bedrooms, a queen-sized bed in each, and nothing else. The living room is just as I saw it yesterday, without much character, with minimalist furniture, and on the kitchen counter, there's that sole pacifier. Next to it is a Post-it note.

The note reads:

*Found under the counter. Didn't know if someone had missed it.*

I swallow, both mortified and heartbroken. I didn't come here to cause a scene. I came here for my baby. Nothing I wanted has been accomplished.

As I walk back to the porch empty-handed, I open my mouth, my words so soft they are nearly still. "I'm sorry. I'm so embarrassed."

"Don't be," Nancy says. "Ivan told us you've been having a hard time." The way she says it tells me Ivan noted a little more than that.

"I'm fine," I say. "Let's just go home, Ivan."

Ivan gives Rob a handshake and Nancy a nod. Then he wraps an arm around me and leads me home.

He's playing the part of a supportive partner, but I know he is holding back. He doesn't bring up the hospital on the walk to the cabin. He doesn't say it's time to check me into a ward.

But I feel it.

I feel that charge, that fear. But he's not the only one terrified.

I am, too, because maybe I've got this all wrong.

Maybe Park is mine.

Maybe the problem isn't him.

Maybe the problem is me.

# CHAPTER ELEVEN

The next day, I'm alone with Park in the bedroom, changing his diaper, when I notice how hot he is, burning up.

"Ivan, hurry," I call out. "Something's wrong."

A moment later, he's in the bedroom with his mason jar of green juice, wearing a post-workout glow. "What's wrong?" he asks, frowning.

"Park. He's so hot. Something's wrong. I think he has a fever."

"Mags," he says, "I'm sure everything's fine."

"I'd ask Melody, but she left, and now—"

"Honey, are you crying?"

"Well, look at him. Feel him." Ivan leans down and presses a hand to the baby's chest. Park looks up at him, astonished, mesmerized. My heart contracts. "Doesn't he feel warm?"

"Maybe." Ivan shrugs. "Look, I don't know a lot about babies. This is the first one I've ever had."

My lips fall into a firm line. "That's one way to put it," I say tightly.

"I'm not putting it any way. I know we've had a baby. I just—"

"It's fine," I say. "You're right. This is our baby here, breathing, living, happy." I give Ivan a bit of a maniacal grin to prove how unaffected I am by his careless words. "And so you're saying Park's fine if he's burning up, then?"

"I'm not saying anything. I just told you I don't know what's wrong with him because I don't really know anything about babies, and Melody's not here. So if you want to take a ferry over and ask Hollis for advice, I can call her up or maybe Thea."

"No, Thea's gone today. She goes to Orcas for her mommy-and-me class."

"All right, so where do you want to go? What do you want to do? Call a pediatrician?"

"Let's go see Hollis. I'm sure the people at the clinic will have an idea if there's something up with him or not."

"Okay," Ivan says. "I'll shower, and we can go on the next ferry. That sound good?"

I pick up Park, cradling him against my chest. "Park," I coo, "are you okay? Are you sick?"

"Mags," Ivan says, shaking his head, and I could finish his sentence; he thinks I'm the one who's sick.

When we get to the Homewood Midwifery Clinic, I'm as tense as I was when I first brought up the fever. "Did you take his temperature?" Hollis asks me when I get into the waiting room.

"Well, no," I say, "I just put my hand on his forehead and chest."

"All right," she says, "Maybe he's just warm. Maybe he had too many blankets on him or something."

"Doesn't he seem flushed, though?"

"He's a baby, Magnolia."

"Well, it's not like you have a baby. Maybe you don't know either."

"Hey." Hollis frowns. "That's pretty harsh."

"Sorry," I say. I know that Hollis would have loved the chance to be a mom.

When Hollis was a teenager, she was driving the car that got her and her sister, Yardley, into a tragic accident. They were both severely injured. Hollis has burn scars along her face, neck and chest. Her sister sustained internal injuries. Hollis had confided in me that when she was younger, she was too insecure to ever look for a partner, and now she says she's too set in her own ways to try again.

She would've been an incredible mother. She's kind and generous and is good at taking care of people. That's why she's such a wonderful midwife. But I know tossing in her face the fact that she doesn't have a baby is cruel and below me.

"I'm so sorry," I repeat. "It was inappropriate. I've just—"

"I know," Hollis says, wrapping her arms around me. "I know." She gives me a big, deep hug, holding on tight, and I lean into it, tears flooding my eyes.

"You think Park's okay?" I ask.

"I think he's fine. But I don't think you're doing so great," she says slowly, carefully choosing her words.

"I know," I say. "I don't mean to be like this."

"Maybe coming here, rushing to make sure Park was okay, is your mind helping you heal. Maybe you're growing more attached to him, and that's a good thing, isn't it?"

"Yeah," I say. "You're right. I mean, I want Park to be happy. I just . . ."

"Yes, keep repeating that. You want Park to be happy, and I want you to be happy too. Is everything okay with you and Ivan?"

I frown. "Why wouldn't it be?"

"I don't know. A new baby in the house, Melody's been around. I want to ensure things are good for you because I love you. After all, you're like a sister to me."

"Things are great with Ivan. He's been checking his phone a lot, but maybe he's just antsy not to be at work."

"Doomscrolling?" Hollis asks with a smirk.

God, I hope he's not doing that. "No," I say. "He's pretty optimistic, and he loves Park, and he loves me."

Hollis smiles. "See? Everything's going to be okay."

"Do you mind watching him for a second? I'm going to use the restroom."

"Of course. Take all the time you need."

In the restroom, I splash cool water on my face, wondering if Hollis is right, if this is all in my head and if maybe being worried about Park's fever is a blessing in disguise. Maybe that is the maternal part of me finally coming out. Maybe it just needed a week to blossom.

As I step back into the hall, I hear Donna, the other midwife from the clinic, speaking to Clover. I slip into the open office door, wanting to listen in. "It's just awful," Clover says. "Billie is so heartbroken about losing her baby, and it's like, can Shaw Island catch a break? A year ago, it was Magnolia. It's so heartbreaking."

I hear Donna's raspy voice. "I know. They're both resilient women, but losing a baby will break anybody."

"You think Billie's broken?"

"I think she needs someone to talk to. Her boss, Tori, wants the best for her, of course, but she's pretty worn out. She has a whole life of her own to deal with."

"And has anyone heard from Hudson, Billie's partner?"

"Ex-partner," Donna clarifies. "No, I don't think so."

"So she's just all alone in her apartment?"

"Sounds like it," Donna finishes.

I exhale slowly, the sorrow over everything Billie is going through pumping through my heart. As I exit the office, I notice a pile of laundered items in a basket. Swaddling blankets mostly, but a tiny cream-colored knit cap is tucked between them. I pull it from the stack, running my fingers over the soft yarn. I know this hat. I made it.

Did Hollis or Clover take it by accident the morning after I gave birth? I frown, wondering how they could have, because when Ivan walked into the bedroom with Park, he wasn't wearing the hat I had put on my infant's head. I remember thinking that it must have been misplaced, or worse, when someone took my baby, they took the cap too.

Holding it in my hands now, I feel a wash of confusion; my memories seem disjointed and fragmented. The power had been out that night, and I couldn't see what cap I put on my daughter — yet I feel in my gut it was this very one I hold now.

I stuff it into my purse before heading back to the lobby, where Hollis is rocking Park.

"He really is adorable," she coos.

"I know," I say, taking him back from her and placing him in the sling. "Hey, I was going to ask you . . . how is Billie doing?"

Hollis sighs. "Everyone's talking about it. We feel so bad for the girl."

"I think it's odd that you never mentioned it to me, considering we gave birth on the same day, that you came from her to me."

Hollis's face falls. "How could I? You were distraught. The night had been so awful. I had been through hell with poor Billie."

"You had a lot on your mind, then, huh?"

"Yeah," she says. "It's not exactly great for the midwifery business, is it?"

"Was it a stillbirth?"

She nods. "Yes."

"Same as me, then," I say, my voice an echo.

"I know, Mags," Hollis says. "I'm so sorry; it's why I didn't want to mention it."

"It's not your fault."

"Just, you've gone through a lot this week too."

"Yeah, I guess a lot of us have. Do you think she'd ever want to talk?" I ask.

"Billie?" Hollis frowns. "Probably not. I think she's pretty fragile right now."

"Oh," I say, surprised at this response. "I kind of thought since we'd both been through . . ."

"No, no, of course. It's just . . . it's all so fresh," Hollis says. "I think you should give it some time."

"Right," I say. "Time." With that, I look at my watch. "Speaking of, I should probably get back to the car. Ivan's waiting for us so we can catch the next ferry home."

"All right," she says. "Look, don't feel bad about over-thinking things with Park. He's a little guy. If you have any concerns or cares, call the pediatrician. That's what you have one for."

"I know," I say. "I will. I just . . . I wanted to see you. I trust you, you know?"

"I know. That's what friends are for."

I gave her one last hug before walking out of the clinic, wishing that the weight in my stomach didn't feel so much like lead.

# CHAPTER TWELVE

When I return to the house, my mind is reeling. I know something's wrong. I know Ivan will not listen or understand, but that doesn't change the fact that I've got to do something. Park and my daughter depend on it.

The knit cap in my diaper bag only confirms what I have felt to be true since the night of the rainstorm.

My daughter was taken from me, and I'm not crazy.

For so long, I've doubted myself and couldn't trust myself about anything. After losing Lucy, my whole world became an emotional landmine. Everything could trip me up. Walking around my house, the very place I had imagined raising my child the entirety of my pregnancy, felt like daggers. The nursery I had painted, the crib Ivan had built, the cradle we had chosen.

Each item of baby clothing, each journal entry I had written on thick cream paper chronicling my pregnancy, memories I hoped my child would read about one day with joy, with love. Then, of course, the pregnancy ended in heartbreak. The delivery, the single worst moment of my life, when she came into the world too late or too soon, it didn't matter.

It wasn't to be.

She was gone before I even had a chance to look into her bright eyes and see a face that mirrored my own. Since I didn't have that choice, I fell apart in the agony of what may have been had it not ended so horribly.

Of course I ended up in the psych ward. I felt everything so deeply, so strongly. I couldn't cope. And as much as I love Ivan and appreciate the man he is, he couldn't understand the pain I felt.

I lost myself in my grief, and then it was no longer processing her death; it was about pretending it had never happened. I understand why I was checked in, why Dr. Bryerson took over my care, why I was medicated and why I roamed the halls of that psych ward for two months straight as everyone around me attempted to get my head back on the way it was supposed to be.

*Supposed to be.* It's a joke, right? What is anything supposed to be anyway?

"You there?" Ivan asks as we pull up to our cabin once we're back at the island. Our home.

"I'm here," I say. "Park seems like he's sleeping, huh?" I say, looking over my seat at the baby carrier in the back. "He's out cold."

"Yeah," Ivan says. He gave him a bottle on the ferry, and now he's out. I didn't think parenting would be this easy. I give him a tight smile, feeling so disconnected from him.

This isn't easy, and this isn't parenting. This is taking care of someone else's baby. But I keep those words swallowed up.

"Hey," I say to him, resting my hand on his, where it sits on the gearshift. "Would you mind taking Park in? I'm going to go into town and get us some dinner, some take-out. I'm dying for some curry."

Ivan smiles. "Oh yeah? I could go in if you want, or we could all drive."

"No," I say. "Don't worry about it. Go in with Park. Maybe he'll stay asleep in the car seat for a while. You could always follow up on those nanny recommendations that Thea gave us."

He smiles, leaning in for a kiss. I oblige.

"Do you want your regular tikka masala with chicken?"

"You know me well," he says, opening the driver's door.

I open my door, too, and take the driver's seat as he grabs Park from the back. "I love you," I say.

"Oh, can you grab some of that garlic naan too? That stuff's so good."

"I got it," I tell him.

I watch until they're safely inside the cabin, and then I reverse the car, headed to town.

It's not that I want to lie to him, trick him, sneak around him, even, but I do need some clarity, and I'm not going to get it by talking to him or Hollis or Thea.

I need to talk to Billie.

I know Ivan will be concerned when I don't show back up at the house immediately, but I don't care. I hightail it to the ferry terminal, thankful these boats run every thirty minutes and the ride is only fifteen.

Once I get off the boat onto Orcas, I drive to the café downtown. I park the car and head inside, knowing I only have so much time before the next ferry boat leaves. I see the owner I've met before, waiting on a customer at the front register.

"Hey," I say. "I was wondering if Billie is working today?"

She shakes her head. "Oh, no, Billie is off for a while." She looks at me and then smiles. "Are you Magnolia, the midwife over at Homewood?"

I nod. "Yeah, I am. I was talking to Hollis, who delivered Billie's baby, and . . . anyway, I just thought I'd stop by and say hi to her."

She nods slowly, and I know what she's doing. She's putting pieces together. She's remembering. I lost my baby too.

I watch her as she processes this until she eventually gives me a small smile. "You know, Billie's upstairs. I could text her and let her know you want to come by?"

"That would be great. I just want her to feel less alone."

She smiles softly. "Well, I know she could use that. She's been taking all of this very rough, which I understand. It is rough. It's . . ." She swallows. "I don't need to explain that to you."

"No," I tell her. "You don't."

A few minutes later, I've climbed the back steps to the apartment over the café. I knock, and Billie opens the door. She's young, early twenties, maybe, with a black bob and severe bangs, pale skin, hollow eyes and tear-streaked cheeks. "Hey," she says, her voice barely a whisper. "I wasn't expecting company."

"You don't need to do anything on my account. I don't even need to come in. I just . . ."

She shrugs. "It's fine," she says, pulling the door open. "At this point, it doesn't matter. I don't care who sees me like this."

She sweeps her hand over the apartment. It's small, with take-out containers on the coffee table. "I haven't really left the couch all week."

"That's understandable," I say.

"Hollis told me you lost a baby too," she says softly. "Last year?"

I nod. "Yeah," I tell her. "A little girl named Lucy. She was stillborn."

Billie swallows. "That was the same with my boy," she says. "What I can remember of it, I mean."

I sit down on her couch next to her. She pushes away some throw pillows, making space.

"What do you mean, what you can remember?" I ask.

"Well, the labor was pretty rough, and it all happened really fast. I had called Hollis, telling her I was having contractions, and then she came a few hours later, and I hardly remember anything. I keep coming in and out. I was not really with it."

"What do you mean?" I ask. Hollis's labor and deliveries are unmedicated. She can only give small amounts of pain relief, and even an epidural, if you were at the hospital, wouldn't make you forget things.

"I passed out," she said. "I don't know; I've never been pregnant before. It seemed so much more difficult than I expected." She twists her lip. "Was it hard for you too?"

I remember the first time. It was so exciting, so incredible. Everyone was there from the clinic. The labor was going so well at first, effortless. I was breathing through everything, just like I'd practiced, and things changed quickly. The umbilical cord was tight around her neck. The baby was coming too fast, too hard. I don't want to tell this to Billie, however. I hardly want to remember it myself.

Tears are in my eyes, and Billie reaches out, taking my hand. "I'm sorry. I'm not trying to have you relive the past. I don't even know what my present is. I'm just a mess. I'm sorry."

"Don't apologize, Billie," I say. "It's all a lot to process. I'm still processing it."

She frowns. "I heard you went to the hospital afterward."

"Yeah, I didn't cope so well with losing her. That's why I wanted to check in on you to see how you were dealing with the loss of your son."

"It just feels surreal," she tells me. "I never even wanted to get pregnant. I was thinking I would get an abortion, but then my boyfriend at the time was so insistent, and so I went along with it, and then I fell in love with the baby, you know, once I started feeling him kicking and everything. It felt like, okay, maybe this is going to be okay. We're going to be okay."

Tears spill down Billie's cheeks, the pain so fresh, the memories at the surface.

She finds more words. "And then he was gone, and nothing is okay. Nothing's okay at all. I got one look at him before I fell back asleep. I was so tired. That night was so weird, right? The rainstorm, and the power was out."

"It was weird," I say slowly. "I gave birth by myself."

"Oh wow," she says.

"And to be honest, I don't remember a lot of the after either. After I gave birth, I cleaned up the baby, wrapped her in a blanket, and I woke up, like, five, six hours later, which,

93

in and of itself, is strange, right?" I am processing out loud with Billie for the first time. "What new mother falls asleep that long with an infant next to them?" I shake my head. "It makes me question my maternal instincts."

Billie frowns. "At least you woke up with a baby. I woke up to nothing."

"I'm so sorry," I say, squeezing her hand. "I wish I could do something to make it feel better."

"It's all right," she says. "I guess I'll hold on to that one look, that one memory of him in my arms, forever. God, he was so perfect. He had this cute little nose. He had so much black hair. His eyes were big like mine, and his hair was the same as mine. I felt like, oh, this is my mini-me . . . and then Hollis told me he wasn't breathing, and I started to panic, of course. He was kicking his little legs. He had this birthmark on his thigh."

I pause. "He wasn't stillborn?" I ask.

She shakes her head. "No, he was alive. I know he was. It's just . . ." She starts crying. Her shoulders shake. "That's what makes it so terrible. I wasn't even there for him when he took his last breath. I wasn't even . . ." She continues sobbing, and I pull her to my chest.

"Oh, Billie," I say, but inside, my mind is whirling, racing. If her baby was alive before she fell asleep, how can she be so certain it passed?

"So, you never saw your son after he . . ."

She shakes her head. "I was pretty loopy, and I remember Hollis telling me that there was a problem, that the baby wasn't breathing, and I asked her what she meant, but then I fell asleep. Maybe it's for the best, you know? Not to have experienced it firsthand, the agony. But then Hollis did, of course, and that feels just as horrible, the idea that she had to experience life and death all in the same night."

"You don't need to apologize for that," I tell her. "You didn't do this. You did nothing."

"Maybe not," she says. "But now I guess we'll never really get a chance to know. My baby is gone."

"And you said he had a birthmark?"

She frowns. "Yeah. Why?"

"Where was it, again?"

At this, she looks puzzled, like I'm pressing for a detail that isn't mine to ask about. "On his right thigh," she says. "About the size of a quarter. It's funny because I have one right there too. How weird is that?"

"Weird," I say.

She wipes her eyes. "I'm glad you came by."

"I'm not sure I was much help," I tell her.

"You were," she says. "I felt so alone, but at least you understand."

I hug her before pulling out my phone and sending her my contact information.

"Call if you ever want to talk. I'm not far. I'm right on Shaw Island, and I've been through it."

She smiles sadly. "I wish that's not what brought us together."

"Me too," I tell her. "Me too."

After I get the curry, I drive home, replaying the conversation in my head. The doubt that I'd felt before is bubbling up in a way I can't contain.

The birthmark, the knit cap, the fact her son was alive when she fell asleep and gone when she woke.

It doesn't add up.

I need to find my daughter, because Billie deserves to have her son home.

# CHAPTER THIRTEEN

When I get in the house with the bag of curry, I notice Ivan quickly shoving his phone in his jeans pocket before turning to me as I walk into the kitchen. I assume he is going to ask where I've been, considering I've been gone for nearly two hours.

"Everything okay?" I ask.

"Of course," he says. "It's great." He comes closer and kisses me on the cheek, not even mentioning the late hour. "It smells good."

The fact that he doesn't mention that I've taken an extremely long time to get curry has me slightly confused. That's not like him. He's usually on top of those sorts of things, especially this last year with my mental health issues. I wouldn't say he hovers, but I do feel like there are always close tabs kept on me.

"Everything okay with work and taking time off?" I ask as I begin unpacking the bag. He walks over to the swing in the corner and picks up Park, whose eyes are now open.

He rocks him gently. "Everything's fine with work. No problem there," he says. "I'm lucky that I have such a flexible job."

I smile. "I wonder when I'll go back to work."

He frowns. "I thought you were staying home with the baby for a year."

I shrug. "I don't know. Being back at the clinic this week makes me remember how much I love it."

"I think you need more rest before you go back to work."

I pop open the box of rice and pour some on one of my ceramic plates. "You want to keep me home?"

"It's not that," he says. "I just want to make sure everything's stable."

"Did you find us a nanny?" I ask. "Is that who you were on the phone with before I walked in?"

He shakes his head. "No. Actually, I didn't get a chance to circle back to that yet."

I nod slowly, wondering what he was doing the last few hours, then. "Right," I say. "Well, if we had a full-time nanny, it might help me get back to work sooner."

"And that's what you want," he says with a bit of a cynical look. "I always thought you've been dying to be a mom, to stay at home with the kids and . . ."

"Kids!" I say. "Okay. I've been pregnant for two years straight. Not ready to consider another child, Ivan."

"I wasn't saying that either. I'm just . . ."

"It's fine," I say. "Honestly, we're good."

"On that note," he says, "let's not talk about nannies, or babies, or anything tonight. Let's enjoy our curry, stare at this gorgeous boy and dream about our future."

I smile, but I know it's a tight one, insincere because as I look at him holding Park, I have this horrific, gnawing feeling in the pit of my stomach. This baby belongs with its mother.

"What?" he asks, shaking his head. "There you go again. I feel like I keep losing you."

"It's just . . ." I set the tikka masala on the counter and turn toward him. "Ivan, I know we've talked about this, and you don't like the conversation, but . . ."

"But what?" he groans, clearly frustrated with me.

"But this baby, Park — he isn't ours."

Ivan's whole face tightens. "Why are we going here again? Why are you insisting we—"

"I'm not insisting anything. I'm just telling you. The knit cap that I made and put on our daughter the night she was born, during the rainstorm, I found it at the midwife clinic. It was in Hollis's office. And the birthmark on Park's thigh, Billie's baby, who died, he had a birthmark on his thigh too."

"You're comparing our son to a dead boy. I feel like I should call the doctor."

"No," I say, pressing my hand on his bicep. "I'm not saying that. I'm saying . . . Billie's son didn't die. I think Hollis lied. I think she's making something up."

"Why would Hollis make this up? Why would Hollis do this to you?"

"I don't know why. Maybe it's not to me. Maybe she has other reasons."

"What kind of reasons would she have for taking away your daughter and handing Billie's son to you? This is a small-town midwifery practice. It's not a goddamn baby-swap ring."

"What?"

"What would be the motivation for Hollis to do such a thing?"

I press my lips together. "That's what's making me so crazy, Ivan. I don't know. I'm missing something, but I was just talking to Billie."

"When were you talking to Billie?" he asks, his voice dropping.

"Before I got the food, I was . . . I stopped by her apartment. I've been through this. I wanted her to know she's not alone, and I also wanted . . ."

"To pry into a poor young woman's life. A woman who just lost her baby. You wanted to press her for details about the night her baby died?"

"This isn't fair," I say. "You're twisting things to make it sound like I'm doing something wrong. I'm not. I'm trying to solve the—"

"Solve what? You're an investigative reporter now? No. Get a grip, Mags. You're a mother who's literally at the brink of another mental breakdown."

"Don't," I say. "Don't throw that in my face. What happened after the baby died wasn't my fault. That was . . ."

"No one said it was your fault, but it's happening again. You're spiraling. You're not making any sense. You're—"

"What?" I shake my head. "Crazy? I'm not. Not about this. I'm going to find out if there was another baby born on the San Juan Islands the night of the rainstorm, because if there was, it might mean that my daughter is out there. Our daughter is out there, and don't you want to know that? Don't you want the truth?"

"You need to calm down."

"Calm down?" I laugh. "I don't know. Maybe there is something I'm not seeing. Maybe the people at the Airbnb were lying. Maybe there *is* a baby there. There's a pacifier. Maybe they know something. Maybe they're hiding." I turn from hm, heading to the mudroom.

"Where are you going?" he asks.

I shove my feet in my big rain boots, pulling on a thick wool coat. Then I fling open the back door. "I'm going to go back and talk to them."

"Mags, stop it."

"No, you stay here with Park. Eat dinner. I'm going to go. I need answers, and you're not giving them to me."

"So help me God, if you walk out that door, I'm calling Dr. Bryerson. Do you understand me?"

"Fine!" I shout. "Do it. Call whoever you want. I need the truth, and you don't want to listen. I'm going to find an answer. I'm going to find my daughter." I slam the back door, then begin running through the yard.

Maybe I'm throwing a tantrum like a little kid. That's what it must seem like to Ivan, but I'm doing so much more than that. I'm fighting for my child.

I know she's out there somewhere, and I need to know where.

Maybe she's at this Airbnb with Nancy and Rob, and everything's going to be fine.

Maybe she's not, but either way, I need to know, and I'm not going to find out by sitting in my cabin for one more night.

I need answers, and I need them now.

When I get to the Airbnb, I knock on the door.

Nancy answers, concern in her eyes. "I thought we've been over this," she says gently.

Tears fill my eyes, and I blink them away. "I know we have," I say, "and I know you must think I'm crazy, and maybe I am, but I also have a mother's intuition. You're a mom. You must know that."

She nods slowly. "I am a mother. My son just left for college."

"I remember you saying that, and because of that, it makes me think you must understand to some degree that when you feel something in your gut about your child, you're not just going to let it drop."

She exhales slowly. "How can I help you, Magnolia?"

"I just need to know if you're hiding something. If there's a baby in this house. If my baby's here."

"I think the problem," Nancy says, "is that you're talking to the wrong person. If you want to know what happened to the baby, you should talk to whoever was with you at your cabin. They must know more than I do. If you fell asleep, maybe they were awake."

"What do you mean?" I ask. "Who was there that night?"

"There was a car at your house. When I . . . Rob and I turned around. Ask them."

"There was a car down the driveway already?" Nancy nods.

"Yes. Not the car you've been driving. Another one. A Ford Focus."

My stomach drops. "A red one?"

She nods. "Yeah, it was in your driveway. It made it hard to do the turnaround. Anyway, don't you think that they might have a better clue of what was going on in your cabin that night than I do? I have never even been to your house, Magnolia."

"You're saying there was another car in my driveway that night. A black Ford Focus?"

"Yes," she says repeats calmly. "Talk to them."

"Thank you," I say, feeling breathless. My body shakes, my mind reels. There was someone else at the house that night. Someone in a black SUV. "Wait," I say, "and you mean this was in the middle of the night? Not in the morning? Not at eight or nine?"

Nancy shakes her head. "No, it was at maybe four a.m."

"Okay," I say softly. "Thank you."

"I would help you more if I could. I just, I don't know this island. I don't know the people here."

"No, no, it's fine," I say, meaning it. "I appreciate everything, and that helps."

Nancy sighs. "Good luck, Magnolia. Keep me posted."

"Will do, Nancy." I walk away, my eyes staring straight ahead. Rooney told me there were two cars that night, but he didn't say in which order they came in. I assumed Hollis came a lot later. That when he was talking about Hollis's car, it was when she and Clover came. It never entered my mind that Hollis was already at the house, and if she was at the house in the middle of the night . . .

Horror washes over me. There's only one reason Hollis would've been at my house.

I gave birth to a daughter at ten. Billie gave birth to a son at midnight.

Then I fell asleep.

When I woke up, my husband was holding a boy.

Why would Hollis take my baby?

That's what I need to know. And I need to know that now.

# CHAPTER FOURTEEN

Quickly, I make my way back to the house. Now that I have confirmation that Hollis's car was here earlier in the night before Ivan ever came home, it gives me the clarity I need.

Also the heartbreak I was hoping to avoid. Of course I want answers about where my daughter is, but I don't want one of my closest friends to be connected to this conspiracy.

I push my way into the front door, panicked. I know my eyes must be crazed, my hair a mess. My mind is whirling.

Ivan is pacing, on the phone. He shoves the phone away, ending a call the moment he sees me. "Magnolia," he says.

I dial in on him. "Who are you talking to? Is it the doctor that you call Dr. Bryerson? Because you shouldn't do that behind my back!"

"No, it wasn't the doctor. Look, Magnolia, I need to talk to you."

"No, I need to talk to you. Look at me, Ivan. Look at me. I know you think I've lost it. You think I'm crazy, insane, but . . ."

Ivan runs his hands through his hair. "I didn't say that."

"You have said that. All week you've been thinking that, saying as much."

"That's fair," he says. "But I think there's something bigger at play than you realize."

"You think?" I snap, shocked, upset. "That's what I've been trying to tell you for days. Something is very, very wrong. Park isn't our baby, and Hollis had something to do with it."

Ivan's face goes white, slack. "I think I might know what she has to do with all of this," he says.

I search him, wanting to see the man I married five years ago, the man who held my hand when we lost Lucy, the man who held my hand when I found out I was pregnant a second time, the man who'd promised to be my person, my rock, an anchor, all of the above.

I need to see him, know him, believe him.

"What does she have to do with it? I can't seem to put the pieces of the puzzle together."

"I think you've done a pretty good job," he says, pressing his fingertips to his temples. "But what I'm going to tell you, Magnolia, it's going to change things between us forever."

"What do you mean?" I ask, worry washing over me all over again. When will this confusing nightmare end?

Ivan starts to cry. "Well, first I have to come clean."

"Come clean about what?" I ask, not anticipating the direction of the conversation.

"When you were in the hospital all those months ago after we lost Lucy, I was really struggling."

I nod slowly, scanning the room. The Indian food still sits on the counter. Park is tucked into a Moses basket on the floor. The house is calm. Music plays softly in the background. If I could just bottle this up and make it mine forever, it would be a good, happy life.

Except it would be missing so many pieces.

My little girl, for one, and the confession Ivan seems to be on the brink of making.

"What is it?" I ask. "Just tell me. What did you do?"

"I slept with Yardley when you were in the hospital." He covers his hands with his face. "I'm sorry, Magnolia. I'm so, so sorry. It happened."

"Don't tell me," I say, covering my mouth with my hands. "Don't tell me any more. I don't want to know."

"You need to know," he says. "You need to know the truth. I don't understand it all, but I think she and Hollis, they've done something with our daughter."

That gets me to lean in close to look at him again, to pull back my hand and stop being scared.

He may have threatened the sanctity of our marriage, but he hasn't stopped trusting me. "You believe we're missing our daughter?"

He nods slowly. "Look, about six months ago, I started getting these texts from Yardley. We had a one-night stand. That was it. She was there for me when I was at my most vulnerable, utterly broken. I had been at a yoga retreat. You know how she used to constantly come to all my retreats?"

"I remember," I say, nodding.

Some dim memories begin to come back into place. Yardley, Hollis's sister, is a health influencer. She runs an online magazine, and when I first started dating Ivan, she was annoyed. The unspoken story was she'd been interested in him, and he didn't reciprocate. He'd chosen me.

I've never thought of her in that light again, figuring we're on different islands, and she could move on. Maybe she never did.

"Look," he says. "She came to my class. We went out for dinner. We had a bunch to drink. I was so upset, grieving the loss of Lucy, feeling like I'd also lost you. It was wrong. I knew it at the time it was wrong, and yet" — he shakes his head — "I did it anyway. I couldn't tell you, of course, for a hundred different reasons. You were still at the hospital. You were seeing Dr. Bryerson. You were processing so much. I wasn't going to add one more thing that didn't matter at all to your plate. You have to believe me on that, Magnolia, or maybe you don't. It's your life. You can choose to do with it what you will. But know this, I've never thought of Yardley again, but she has thought of me."

"What has she thought?" I ask.

"She told me she was pregnant. This is when you'd already found out you were having a baby, and so I set it aside. The whole prospect of raising her child was absurd, and she never gave me proof. I blocked her number. I told her I didn't want to talk to her, but she kept insisting she was having my baby. So then I was trying to be a good guy. I said, 'Fine, let's meet up. Let me see the ultrasound pictures,' and she refused. At that point, I figured it was all a big scam, right? She was trying to lure me into something that she had no reason doing. I didn't think she was really pregnant. Then a few days ago, I get a text. She says she went into labor. She had a baby."

I frown. "Yardley had a baby? Why didn't Hollis say anything?"

"I don't know. Maybe she was trying to protect you. At least that's what I thought at first. She sent me pictures of our daughter, at least pictures of the baby she had given birth to, said it was a little girl, said she had *just* given birth."

I frown. "I'm still hung up on the fact Hollis kept this from me."

"Well, at first, I thought maybe Hollis was trying to protect you. Maybe she knew that Yardley and I had slept together, but then everything you've been saying about Park, the birthmark, the cap, I heard you."

"Okaaay," I say slowly, trying to process everything my husband is revealing.

"Well, the thing is, I think Hollis took our daughter the night she was born, and I think she swapped it with Park."

I frown. "And you think Hollis, my closest friend, gave my daughter to Yardley? Why would she do this?"

"That's what I'm trying to understand. Why does Hollis owe her sister so damn much that she would be willing to risk so much? Her friendship with you, but also her practice? Why would Hollis feel like she owes Yardley everything?"

My eyes widen, horror wrapping around my heart. "Because Hollis was the one driving the car when they got in an accident all those years ago. The burns and scarring that

Hollis has, she was behind the wheel, and Yardley, she had internal damage. She can never have children. Hollis was driving the car drunk that night, and that choice took away her sister's opportunity to be a mother."

Ivan looks at me astonished. "You think Hollis is doing this to make amends with her sister?"

"If everything you're saying is true, then it's the only answer."

"In that case, we need to go get our baby back."

## CHAPTER FIFTEEN

For the past week, it hasn't felt like anyone has been on my side. Like I was burying this fear, this agony all by myself. Now Ivan and I are in it together. In some messy, complicated, convoluted way, we are in this next part side by side.

Park starts fussing, and I walk to the Moses basket, picking him up. I sit on the couch and unhook my nursing bra, offering him my breast, hating that he's not with his mother. Tears fill my eyes as I try and process it.

I don't know how we're supposed to do this. We need to go get our daughter. We need to get Billie back her son.

My eyes close as tears streak my cheeks, Park suckling happily, and for that, at least, I feel relief. I haven't let this baby down while he's been in my care. I didn't feel as if he was my own, but I didn't stop nurturing him the way he deserves.

My chin quivers as I think about the loss Billie has experienced, one I wouldn't wish on my worst enemy. Especially not her, a young woman feeling as if she's lost everything, when, in fact, it was taken from her.

"I think we should call the police," Ivan says. "Let's talk to Thea's husband and clue him in on this."

I nod. "That seems like the best thing to do. And you're sure Yardley's in on all this?"

He nods. "The pieces fit right."

It all clicks. He pulls his phone from his pocket and calls Thea's husband, Tanner. I guess it helps to have a police officer in town who knows us intimately. And since Thea believed me, or at least put some amount of faith in my story a few days ago, I'm sure she's given Tanner those details too.

I try to focus on Park, on being calm and relaxed for him as Ivan makes his phone call. Maybe the most important call of his life.

A few minutes later, he comes back into the living room.

"Tanner is sending out a team to Yardley's home. I gave him the information, and if all goes well, maybe we'll have a baby here. *Our* baby, by the end of the night."

"And Park?" I say. "What are we supposed to do with him?"

"Well, if we truly believe it's Billie's baby, then . . ."

"There's just one thing that I don't understand. Why go to all this trouble to swap the babies? Why not just give Park to Yardley? Why did Hollis take our daughter?"

At this, Ivan begins to cry. He sits next to me on the couch, his arm around my shoulder.

"Because that's the only way she could prove paternity, right? She must have realized it was all serendipitous. Hollis knew you were in labor, knew Billie was in labor, knew Yardley needed a baby soon if she wanted to keep me. Hollis did what she thought was best for her sister."

I press my lips together. "She's a monster. And to think she's going into people's homes every day, helping them bring their new life in the world when she'd so willingly destroyed so many other people's happiness. It's horrible."

"And now she'll pay."

* * *

Three hours later, Tanner, in uniform, arrives on our doorstep. He is holding a newborn girl in an infant car seat carrier.

The moment I see her, I begin to cry. My shoulders shake, the truth wrapping around me in a way that comforts and scares me.

"Our daughter," I whisper.

Tanner hands me a little girl. "She confessed to everything once confronted with the story. I'm so glad you called me right away. She has her whole apartment packed; she was ready to flee town."

"Oh my God," I say, cradling this little one in my arms. Melody is here, now filled in on the situation, and she gasps at the beauty of this moment.

This mirror of me, my daughter, home at last.

Ivan has Park in a car seat, a diaper bag and plenty of other gear in a tote bag for the officers to take to Billie. She's going to be so horrified, so shocked. So damned happy.

"We have a social worker with her now, preparing her for the news," Tanner explains.

I smile, heartbroken and yet somehow fully alive. "I know we're not owed this information, but considering these tiny infants' lives are on the line, I appreciate it."

Ivan shakes his head. "I hope she does okay with the news. It's all so much."

"Sounds like she has her boyfriend there with her, and I think right now you just need to worry about yourself, Magnolia," Tanner says. "I know Thea plans on calling you tomorrow, but for tonight, you and Ivan and your daughter, it sounds like you guys need to get some rest. You have some reacquainting to do, huh?"

Tanner and the officer with him leave, with Park in the car seat. But before they do, before they go, I tell them to stop. I hand my little girl to her father and lean in front of the car seat one last time. I push back the visor. I look Park in the eyes.

"Hey, sweet pea. You're going to be okay now. You're going to your mama, and I will love you in some way forever."

I kiss his forehead, offering up a prayer for this little soul that whatever happens with him next, his life is good. This little baby came into the world deserving a mother who loved him, and now he will get just that.

I go back into the house with Ivan, who's holding our daughter, swaddled in pink.

"I can't believe this," Melody says. "It's all so shocking."

"Hollis and Yardley are going to go to jail. I can't believe the choices they've made. It's unfathomable."

Ivan looks over at Melody. "Would you mind heading home? I think Magnolia needs a night at home with her daughter."

Melody nods, tears in her eyes. "Of course. And if you need anything, I am always a phone call away." She squeezes my shoulders, kissing me on the cheek, before giving my daughter a long look. "She is perfect. And she is so lucky to have a mom like you."

\* \* \*

After Melody leaves, I walk into the bedroom, my daughter in my arms. "I hope she loves me even though I haven't been with her for a week."

"Don't worry about that tonight," Ivan says, tucking hair behind my ear. "She has the most amazing mama. You are the bravest woman I know."

"You thought I was crazy," I say. I shuffle off my slippers and crawl into bed, my little girl in my arms.

"You haven't even gotten mad at me yet for what I did with Yardley. For . . ."

"Don't," I say. "We've all done things we wish we hadn't. I'm not going to hold anything against you."

"You're too good to me."

"No," I say. "I just had a lot of growing up take place the last few years, and I know life is more complicated than some people give it credit for. So you slept with Yardley. I don't feel like that changes anything. The moment you looked in my eyes and told me you believed me gave me faith in us, and right now, that's enough."

Tears are in Ivan's eyes. "I love you," he says, "and I love her."

We look down at our daughter. "She doesn't even have a name," I say. "A week old, and she doesn't have a name."

Tears fill my eyes as I look her over, that face I memorized that night I gave birth. Ten fingers, ten toes, eyes that are blue, hair that is fair and a nose that matches mine.

"I love you," I say to her. "I love you. I love you. I love you."

Ivan asks me what we should name her. "How about Scout?"

He smiles. "That's a solid name. I think she's going to be a strong girl."

I pull her to my chest, and I offer her my breast. She takes it, and I exhale. My eyes close, my prayer answered. I wanted a daughter, a child, and now I have her, and she is mine, and I will not let her go.

All that has transpired has turned me into an overprotective mama bear. And yes, there's probably not going to be a whole lot of balance happening in this equation for a long while. But I don't care and won't apologize because the mother's intuition is always correct.

I will fight for my girl. Even if people think I'm crazy, I will fight for her no matter what.

Scout's honor.

# EPILOGUE

*One year later . . .*

The clinic is finally slowing down — babies seem to come in batches, and several clients gave birth in the last week. Donna and I are ready for a few days of rest. After Hollis and Yardley were sentenced at trial, Donna and I decided to buy the business ourselves. As co-owners, we hired a new midwife from Seattle, Cady, who brings lots of experience and none of the drama.

Which is what I am craving a lot these days. I work for those stress-free moments of bliss with the people I love.

The bells on the front door jingle as someone enters the clinic. It's Ivan, bringing me Scout. He is headed off to host a yoga retreat, and I am taking Scout to her best friend's house. I know at one you can't choose your best friend, but Billie and I decided on our kiddos for one another.

They were born the same night, and after spending the first week of Park's life caring for him, the bond became something beautiful, and Billie became the sister I never had.

She needed family and a support system, and I was ready to offer my hand.

"Hey, Mags," Ivan says, kissing me. "You look happy."

"I am," I say, taking Scout from his arms. "Did you guys have a nice morning?"

"It was wonderful—"

"Mama, Mama, Mama!" I give her kisses, and she tosses her head back, laughing. Her first word, "mama," will never, ever get old.

"Hey, sweetie, Mama has you now." I squeeze her against my chest.

"Let me help get you both loaded into the car," Ivan says.

I turn and say goodbye to Clover and Cady, both working the clinic this afternoon. They blow Scout air kisses, and she giggles to the car.

Ivan takes her from me and transfers her to the car seat in my vehicle. I give him a hug and a kiss goodbye. "Have a good weekend," I say before he leans down to give our daughter another kiss.

"I will. Oh, and tell Billie hello. Maybe next week, we can have them over for dinner?"

It only takes a few minutes to drive over to Billie's house. Once we get there, I text her to let her know we've arrived.

She responds right away. *We'll be right down!*

I get Scout out of the car and place her in the open stroller, shoving the diaper bag in the basket beneath.

When Billie emerges on the sidewalk with Park — she kept the name Ivan picked for him — she gives Scout and me big smiles.

"Missed you, Mags," she says, giving me a side hug. "Can you hold him a sec while I get the stroller from my car?"

I take her son and give him a big smile. "Hey, little guy, I've missed you."

And I have. I knew he was not my child, but he was with me, in my bed, on my breast, at my side, for the first week of my motherhood. I will always be linked to him.

When Billie returns with the stroller, she gets Park situated, then asks if I want to walk down to Thea's house, as is our Friday afternoon routine. Thea is expecting us, and we've been texted and told that she made pumpkin loaf and has a pot of coffee waiting for us. I smile, grateful for my friendships. Thankful for this life.

Billie and I push our children forward, and I am overwhelmed with a profound sense of peace, knowing I didn't make any mistakes. I followed my intuition and brought both our children home.

## THE END

# THE JOFFE BOOKS STORY

We began in 2014 when Jasper agreed to publish his mum's much-rejected romance novel and it became a bestseller.

Since then we've grown into the largest independent publisher in the UK. We're extremely proud to publish some of the very best writers in the world, including Joy Ellis, Faith Martin, Caro Ramsay, Helen Forrester, Simon Brett and Robert Goddard. Everyone at Joffe Books loves reading and we never forget that it all begins with the magic of an author telling a story.

We are proud to publish talented first-time authors, as well as established writers whose books we love introducing to a new generation of readers.

We have been shortlisted for Independent Publisher of the Year at the British Book Awards three times, in 2020, 2021 and 2022, and for the Diversity and Inclusivity Award at the Independent Publishing Awards in 2022.

We built this company with your help, and we love to hear from you, so please email us about absolutely anything bookish at feedback@joffebooks.com

If you want to receive free books every Friday and hear about all our new releases, join our mailing list: www.joffebooks.com/contact

And when you tell your friends about us, just remember: it's pronounced Joffe as in coffee or toffee!

**ALSO BY ANYA MORA**

**STANDALONES**
MY HUSBAND'S WIFE
NOT MY BABY

Milton Keynes UK
Ingram Content Group UK Ltd.
UKHW011318111223
434168UK00005B/470